Ken Ludwig's

SULLIVAN & GILBERT

A Play with Music

A SAMUEL FRENCH ACTING EDITION

SAMUEL FRENCH

FOUNDED 1830

New York Hollywood London Toronto

SAMUELFRENCH.COM

CHARACTERS

William Schwenck Gilbert - dramatist and lyricist

Sir Arthur Sullivan - composer

Richard D'Oyly Carte - impresario/producer of the Savoy
Operas

Lucy Turner (Kitty) Gilbert - Gilbert's wife

Alfred, Duke of Edinburgh - second son of Queen Victoria
and one of Sullivan's best friends

Violet Russell - a young soprano

Francois Cellier - conductor

George Grossmith, baritone)
Rutland Barrington, bass-baritone)
Durward Lely, tenor)
Courtice Pounds, tenor) principal Savoyards
Rosina Brandram, contralto)
Jessie Bond, mezzo-soprano)
Sybil Grey, soprano)

SULLIVAN & GILBERT was presented by The Kennedy Center for the Performing Arts, The National Arts Centre of Canada and Gemstone Productions during 1988 at The National Arts Centre of Canada, The St. Lawrence Centre for the Arts (Toronto) and The Eisenhower Theatre at The Kennedy Center. It was directed by Leon Major; choreographed by Marcia Milgrom Dodge; the set was designed by Phillip Silver; the costumes were designed by Martha Mann; the lighting was by Peter McKinnon; the musical director was Glenn Morley; the associate musical director was Melody McShane; and the stage manager was Pat Thomas. The cast, in order of appearance, was as follows:

WILLIAM S. GILBERT .... Fritz Weaver
SIR ARTHUR SULLIVAN .... Noel Harrison
LUCY TURNER (Kitty) GILBERT .... Kate Trotter
DURWARD LELY .... Daniel Marcus
COURTICE POUNDS .... Greg Bond
RUTLAND BARRINGTON .... Philip Booth
SYBIL GREY .... Lisa Vroman
JESSIE BOND .... Leslie Toy
ROSINA BRANDRAM .... Christina James
RICHARD D'OYLY CARTE .... Graham Harley
FRANCOIS CELLIER .... Glenn Morley
VIOLET RUSSELL .... Donna English
ALFRED, DUKE OF EDINBURGH .... Edward Duke
GEORGE GROSSMITH .... Walter Hudson
MASTER CARPENTER .... Timothy Cruickshank
MISTRESS OF WARDROBE .... Susan Cuthbert
MISTRESS OF WARDROBE .... Alicia Jeffery
MASTER OF PROPERTIES .... David Playfair

Previous productions were presented by the American Stage Festival, StageArts Theatre Company (Ruth Ann Norris and Nell Robinson) and the Huntington Theatre.

SYNOPSIS OF SCENES

The setting: The action of the play takes place in December,
                  1890, all but the Prologue at the Savoy Theatre,
                  London, England.

ACT ONE

Prologue: Harrow Weald and London, during a week in
                  early December.

Scene 1:   The stage of the Savoy Theatre, the following
                  Saturday at 10 a.m.

Scene 2:   A corridor backstage, immediately following.

Scene 3:   Gilbert and Sullivan's dressing room at the Savoy
                  Theatre, immediately following.

Scene 4:   The Savoy stage, a half hour later.

Scene 5:   A corridor, green room and dressing room
                  backstage, immediately following.

Scene 6:   The Savoy stage, immediately following.

Scene 7:   Gilbert and Sullivan's dressing room, a few
                  minutes later.

ACT TWO

Scene 1:   The Savoy stage, same day, later afternoon.

Scene 2:   Gilbert and Sullivan's dressing room, a few
                  minutes later.

Scene 3:   The Savoy stage, a few minutes later.

Scene 4:   The Savoy stage, immediately following.

Scene 5:   The corridor outside Gilbert and Sullivan's
                  dressing room, an hour later.

Scene 6:   A corridor backstage immediately following.

Epilogue: The Savoy stage, immediately following.

MUSICAL SYNOPSIS

ACT ONE

Prologue:	Brightly Dawns Our Wedding Day, First Verse, (*The Mikado*)
Scene 1:	Medley: I Have a Song to Sing, O! (*The Yeomen of the Guard*) Here's a How-de-do (*The Mikado*) Sad is That Woman's Lot (*Patience*) In Sailing O'er Life's Ocean Wide (*Ruddigore*) Poor Wand'ring One (*The Pirates of Penzance*) Dance a Cachucha (*The Gondoliers*) I Am a Maiden Cold and Stately (*Princess Ida*)
Scene 4:	When You're Lying Awake (*Iolanthe*) If You Go In (*Iolanthe*)
Scene 6:	Young Man Despair (*The Mikado*) So Please You Sir (*The Mikado*) Three Little Maids From School (*The Mikado*)

ACT TWO

Scene 1:	Would You Know the Kind of Maid (*Princess Ida*) Never Mind the Why and Wherefore (*H.M.S. Pinafore*)
Scene 3:	I Know a Youth Who Loves a Little Maid (*Ruddigore*) When I Go Out of Door (*Patience*)
Epilogue:	Brightly Dawns Our Wedding Day, Second Verse, (*The Mikado*) For He's Gone and Married Yum-Yum (*The Mikado*) The Threatened Cloud Has Passed Away (*The Mikado*)

The Orchestra

In the 1988 tour of *Sullivan & Gilbert,* we had eleven musicians and three synthesizers in the pit. In a 1985 Off Broadway production presented in a small theatre on 38th Street in New York, the orchestra consisted of one old piano and one very versatile piano player. It was clear that the audiences enjoyed the productions equally, which suggests that the piece works equally well with as many (or as few) musicians as the budget allows.

Stagehands

In virtually all productions of the play to date, the understudies (and in some cases theatre apprentices) were costumed as Victorian stagehands (carpenters, wardrobe ladies, etc.) and included in the action of the piece wherever appropriate. This generally included the scenes taking place on the Savoy stage. The advantage of this approach was three-fold. First, it added immeasurably to the feeling of life backstage. Second, it allowed sets and props to be set and struck in front of the audience, in character, and therefore helped to avoid pauses between scenes. Third, the stagehands joined in the choruses of the bigger production numbers (sometimes from the wings), which of course added to the sound. Also, if the budget permits, the stagehands could be costumed for the *Mikado* finale to make the final moment as grand as possible.

Action

It's important for the rhythm of *Sullivan & Gilbert* that the scenes of the play flow from one to the next as seamlessly as possible. This will to some extent be a function of the set. But it will mostly be a function of the director's ingenuity and imagination. For example, in the 1988 production, the transition from scene one to scene two in Act One was enhanced by having George Grossmith cross the stage at an angle wearing his jaunty overcoat (he's just arriving at the theatre) declaiming the first stanza of *A Modern Major General.* Simultaneously, the scene one set was disappearing and the corridor for scene two (a simple flat with lights) was moving into place. As noted above, this and most of the other transitions were also aided by the Victorian stagehands. In brief, the director should use whatever means he has at his disposal to make each act flow continuously.

[MUSIC CUE #1: MADRIGAL (a cappella)]

ACT I

Prologue

The performance begins with the first verse of the madrigal "Brightly Dawns Our Wedding Day" from "The Mikado", sung a capella in the darkness.

London and Harrow Weald.

December, 1890.

WILLIAM SCHWENCK GILBERT and SIR ARTHUR SULLIVAN are revealed standing at opposite sides of the stage, each in his own pool of light. Behind each man is a chair, and beside each chair is a telephone. GILBERT is at Grim's Dyke, his home outside London on the Harrow Weald; SULLIVAN is at Queen's Mansions, his home on Victoria Street, London. The settings should be simple but evocative.

Both men are at the heights of their careers and appear to be in their mid-fifties. About them clings the success that comes with age and work. Where GILBERT is rumpled, sturdy and gruff, SULLIVAN is of a gentler spirit, a man of elegance and high-strung sensitivity.

GILBERT. One December, 1890. Dear Sullivan —

(The light on SULLIVAN fades, making GILBERT the focus of interest.)

9

GILBERT. As I have promised to leave off the subject of our quarrel, I see no cause for your entreating me to do so one letter after another. As far as I am concerned, the subject is closed. (*Pause.*) Let me only remind you that if D'Oyly Carte had consented to my examining the books – into which it is not unreasonable to suppose that certain errors may have crept, elfin and innocent – no legal proceedings would have been taken! Nothing more. I am finished. (*Pause.*) Now, how are you feeling? Needless to say, if your health remains fragile you shall *not* conduct opening night and that is that. The rehearsals, since you ask, are proceeding on schedule. What with our first revue, and the Queen coming, there is a delightful edge in the air; and with all of the principals doing their most famous bits, the hamming is beyond rational belief. We have one new girl, a soprano named Violet Russell. Otherwise it's the old-timers. Grossmith, Jessie, Sybil, the lot. Except, of course, for Leonora. How sad that she is gone forever. (*Pause.*) Married. When she told me, I called her a little fool for leaving the company. To which she says, "You make such fun of old women. Well, I shall be old soon. Will you provide for me? No!" she says, "So I'm going to a man who will!" The wheel is turning, Sullivan, and the children marry. It is fortunate that neither of us ages. Yours truly, W.S. Gilbert. P.S. How is your liver? My gout is doing tremendously well. It is now up to my arms.

(*Light up on SULLIVAN, fade on GILBERT.*)

SULLIVAN. Four December. Dear Gilbert – Again I beg of you to leave the subject of the accounts. I assure you that I have not yet got over the shock of seeing our names coupled, not in brilliant collaboration over a work destined for world-wide celebrity, but in hostile antagonism over a few miserable pounds. As for the review, I *shall* conduct opening night if I have to do it from a bath chair. (*Pause.*) Incidentally, I showed the present selection of the songs to Alfred, and he feels, as I do, that we're a little short on ballads, which, by the by he tells me, are the Queen's favorites. What do you think? Now for the real news. Brace yourself. As you know, I have always longed to find someone as wonderful as your Kitty. Well, I've found her. The "right woman." I know of course what you're going to say, but this time it's different, I assure you. She's younger than I am, very beautiful, and gay as a breeze. Then, too, she can be horribly stubborn, which is when — don't laugh — she reminds me of you. I can't tell you her name yet, so please don't ask, but ... (*Deliberately, with relish.*) ... I am quite sure you know her. Enough of this. I am a schoolboy again! Love to Kitty. Yours ever sincerely, A. Sullivan. P.S. Did you get your telephone yet? They are such fun. The problem is, until more of them are sold, there's no one to call.

(*Light up on GILBERT, fade on SULLIVAN.*)

GILBERT. Seven December. Dear Sullivan — Who is she? You might as well tell me at once, as I shall pry it out of you in any case. And of course you need my approval, since you are senile and therefore under age. Whoever she is, marriage, of course, is a dangerous business, as any husband can tell you. Your first child — whom you shall name after me, boy or girl — will regularly crawl into your piano and throw up. If I may change the subject, I can hardly believe that you had the gall to show my script to your "friend" Alfred, the Duke of Edinburgh. In my opinion, the man has the musical acumen of an organ grinder and less brains than the monkey. Not being knighted as you are, I am not over-solicitous of the Queen's whims. Because I take our joint work seriously, I do not ask my friends if they approve of your music, and I expect the same courtesy. Yours truly, W.S. Gilbert. P.S.

My telephone was installed last week. I shall be happy to receive a call from you at your convenience.

(*Light up on SULLIVAN. Both lights remain up through the end of the scene.*)

SULLIVAN. Dear Gilbert – I am not surprised that you do not ask your friends if they approve of my music. You don't have any. I shall ring you on the 12th at about 5:30. Will you be there? A.S.

GILBERT. Dear Sullivan – I had one friend, but he died. He fell asleep listening to your "Imperial March" and no one could wake him. This may also come as a surprise, but one does not make an appointment to use one's own telephone. They are meant, I believe, to be vehicles of spontaneity. If I am not at home when you ring, I shall make it a point not to answer. W.S.G.

(*SULLIVAN, ruffled by Gilbert's irony, sits in his chair, picks up his telephone and clicks for the operator.*)

SULLIVAN. Hello? Operator? How are you? Good. I would like to speak, please, with a Mr.Gilbert in Harrow Weald. William Schwenck,* but don't call him Schwenck, because he doesn't like it. No, I don't have his number, but he lives in a large stone house ... Thank you.

(*Gilbert's telephone rings, and he picks it up.*)

GILBERT. Hello?
SULLIVAN. (*Shouting to bridge the miles.*) GILBERT?
GILBERT. Sullivan?
SULLIVAN. IS THAT YOU?
GILBERT. Stop *shouting!*

---

* Pronounced "Shvenk."

SULLIVAN. WHAT?
GILBERT. Stop SHOUTING!!
SULLIVAN. Sorry.
GILBERT. That's better.
SULLIVAN. Sorry.
GILBERT. Well how are you?
SULLIVAN. Much better. Thank you. How are you?
GILBERT. Fine, fine. Now who is she? This time.
SULLIVAN. Who?
GILBERT. The girl, who is the girl?
SULLIVAN. Oh. I can't tell you.
GILBERT. Of course you can. You won't tell me.
SULLIVAN. I'm sworn to silence. Would you have me betray her confidence?
GILBERT. Yes. Of course.

(KITTY, Gilbert's wife, now enters Gilbert's stage area. In her late thirties, she's a handsome and capable woman who understands every bone in her husband's body, having been married to him since she was seventeen. Her entrance does not at all halt the flow of the Sullivan-Gilbert dialogue, but rather turns it into a trio.)

KITTY. Who is it?
GILBERT. *(To KITTY.)* Arthur.
SULLIVAN. Is that Kitty?
GILBERT. How many wives do you think I have?
KITTY. *(Shouting into the phone.)* HELLO, ARTHUR!
SULLIVAN. HELLO, KITTY!
GILBERT. Stop shouting!
KITTY. Let me talk to him.
GILBERT. Is she tall or short?
SULLIVAN. Hm? Oh, medium I suppose.
GILBERT. Blond or dark?
SULLIVAN. Very blond.
GILBERT. Blond ...

KITTY. Blond?

GILBERT. I've got it! Oh-h, you devil –

KITTY. Who?!

GILBERT. You dog –

SULLIVAN. Come come –

GILBERT. So – you'll have a duke for a father-in-law. (*Ruefully.*) I knew you'd do well.

KITTY. William – !

SULLIVAN. Who?

GILBERT. Helen Locksley, you dog. Admit it!

KITTY. Helen?

SULLIVAN. Helen? Oh - Oh, my God no! (*Laughing.*) Gilbert, she looks like Benjamin Disraeli!

KITTY. Is it Helen?

SULLIVAN. (*Laughing up a storm.*) Helen Locksley. Oh, heavens ...

GILBERT. So it's not bloody Helen Locksley! Dammit!

SULLIVAN. Sorry.

GILBERT. (*Into the phone.*) Here. Laugh at Kitty for a change. (*He hands her the phone.*)

KITTY. Arthur?

SULLIVAN. (*Standing up.*) Kitty, my dear, how are you?

KITTY. Fine, Arthur, and we're so pleased for you.

SULLIVAN. Thank you, dear.

KITTY. Now you must bring her to dinner. As soon as you want to.

GILBERT. (*Yelling into the phone.*) YOU CAN PUT A BAG OVER HER HEAD!

SULLIVAN. We'll come soon, I promise. I know you'll like her.

KITTY. Oh I'm sure I will. We both will.

GILBERT. (*Crossly.*) Give me the phone.

KITTY. (*To GILBERT.*) In a minute! (*To SULLIVAN.*) I knew it wasn't Helen, Arthur. She has a sister, though, a real beauty. Her name is Enid, I think –

GILBERT. (*Yelling into the phone.*) SHE'S GETTING OFF NOW!

KITTY. Here's William back. I'll call you myself.

SULLIVAN. Good! When he's out.

KITTY. Oh Arthur, we do miss seeing you.

SULLIVAN. Me too –

KITTY. Take care of yourself.

SULLIVAN. I will. I promise. (*GILBERT takes the phone from KITTY.*) Good-bye, my dear.

GILBERT. It's me. (*Pause.*) I've got to go now.

SULLIVAN. Oh ... Right.

(*Pause. KITTY smiles at GILBERT wistfully, then exits.*)

GILBERT. So I'll see you Saturday. You will be there?

SULLIVAN. Oh yes. It's almost a year, isn't it?

GILBERT. Nine months.

SULLIVAN. Almost ten, I think.

GILBERT. We'll have a reunion.

SULLIVAN. Yes. (*Pause.*) See you then.

GILBERT. Right. Saturday. (*Sadly.*) Bye.

SULLIVAN. *Sadly.*) Good-bye.

(*They both hang up and look at their telephones as the lights fade.*)

[MUSIC CUE #2: ORCHESTRA TUNING]

Scene 1

The stage of the Savoy Theatre, London.
Saturday, ten a.m.
As the lights are fading on GILBERT and SULLIVAN, the Savoy stage takes life. The silence following

Sullivan's "Good-bye" is split by the sound of the orchestra tuning up. Meanwhile, GILBERT turns and stalks onto the Savoy stage, joining the milieu of the Saturday morning rehearsal. As he does, SULLIVAN and KITTY disappear unobserved into the wings.

The following dialogue, up to the first number, runs rapidly. There should be several centers of interest.

One of the first sounds we hear is DURWARD LELY, a tenor, vocalizing. He enters with COURTICE POUNDS, also a tenor, who is doing voice exercises. Simultaneously, RUTLAND BARRINGTON, a hefty bass-baritone, enters separately from the other side. All three men are in street clothes.

DURWARD. AHHHHH ...

COURTICE. (*Voice exercise.*) Pickadilly, Pickadilly, Pickadilly ...

RUTLAND. (*Eating an apple.*) Good morning.

DURWARD. Morning.

COURTICE. Morning.

RUTLAND. Good morning, William.

GILBERT. If you say so. Where's Carte?

COURTICE. I haven't seen him.

DURWARD. (*Pointing off left.*) He's checking props.

GILBERT. You have five minutes, gentlemen. And don't waste your voices.

(*As GILBERT exits, JESSIE BOND, mezzo-soprano, and SYBIL GREY, soprano, both in street clothes, hurry onstage together. JESSIE is eagerly reading a newspaper, which SYBIL wants desperately to look at.*)

SYBIL. Jessie!

JESSIE. In a second!

SULLIVAN. Don't hog it!

RUTLAND. Good morning.

DURWARD. Morning.
COURTICE. Morning.
JESSIE. Good morning!
SYBIL. Jessie –!
JESSIE. Listen! (*Reading.*) "Tonight at the Savoy Theatre, the D'Oyly Carte Opera Company will present their first revue. In attendance at the opening will be Her Majesty, the Queen!"
SYBIL. Oh God! I can't stand it!
COURTICE. Are there any pictures?
DURWARD. (*Trying to grab it.*) Let's see!
JESSIE. For heaven's sake!

(*By this time, ROSINA BRANDRAM, a contralto of vast proportions, has entered.*)

ROSINA. Good Morning.
COURTICE. Morning.
SYBIL. Morning.
RUTLAND. Good morning, dear.
ROSINA. The *Times*?
SYBIL. She's hogging the whole thing.
JESSIE. *I* bought it.
ROSINA. I read it at breakfast. It's extremely boring.
JESSIE. "Featured in the production will be Messrs. George Grossmith, Rutland Barrington, Durward Lely, Courtice Pounds – "
COURTICE. Slow down!
DURWARD. Durward Lely.
COURTICE. And Courtice Pounds.
JESSIE. "Miss Rosina Brandram, Miss Violet Russell, *and* ... the ever-popular Miss Jessie Bond." Ha! Ever-popular –
SYBIL. What about me?
JESSIE. Hm?
SYBIL. Jessie?!
JESSIE. They seem to have missed you, dear.

SYBIL. (*Grabing the paper.*) I don't believe it! Those idiots!

(*RICHARD D'OYLY CARTE, the seasoned producer and head of the company, has entered by this time, clipboard in hand, busy and on edge.*)

CARTE. Three minutes!
ROSINA. Good morning, Richard.
DURWARD. Morning.
JESSIE. Morning!
RUTLAND. Morning.
SYBIL. Mr. Carte –
CARTE. Not now.
SYBIL. but the papers –
CARTE. Sybil –
SYBIL. But I'm not even mentioned! And they name Violet, and she's only been here six weeks!
CARTE. Sorry, dear. Life is cruel. (*Peering into the pit.*) Cellier? ... Cellier?!

(*FRANCOIS CELLIER, conductor, enters from the wings.*)

CELLIER. Right here!
DURWARD. Morning.
CELLIER. Good morning.

(*At this point, SYBIL, who's been paging through the newspaper, lets out a piercing scream. Everyone stops dead and stares at her.*)

CARTE. Good God! What is it?!
SYBIL. The picture! I'm in the picture! Look!
JESSIE. Where?!
DURWARD. Let's see!
JESSIE. Good shot!
SYBIL. Rosina, look at you!

(JESSIE and SYBIL shriek with laughter. Meanwhile, CELLIER descends into the pit.)

CARTE. You have one minute, ladies. And time is money.
JESSIE. Yes sir.
SYBIL. Yes sir.

(As CARTE exits, VIOLET RUSSELL, a pretty soprano in her early twenties, hurries onstage from the other direction, out of breath. She wears an overcoat and carries a muff, both flattering to her.)

VIOLET. Oh thank goodness!
DURWARD. Morning.
COURTICE. Morning.
VIOLET. Good morning. I thought I was late.
DURWARD. You're looking well.
COURTICE. You shouldn't run, you know. It's bad for the wind.
RUTLAND. Good morning.
VIOLET. Morning.

(By this time, all three men are hovering around VIOLET as if drawn by a magnet.)

JESSIE. *(To SYBIL.)* Well look at that. It's a convention.
SYBIL. Looks more like a mating dance to me.
JESSIE. Good morning, Vi!
SYBIL. Morning!
VIOLET. *(Breaking away from the men.)* Good morning. Big day.
JESSIE. Oh, it's only the Queen.
SYBIL. Same old thing ...
JESSIE. New coat, Vi?
VIOLET. Yes. It is actually.

SYBIL. Very flattering.
JESSIE. It looks expensive.
VIOLET. It – it wasn't, really. I found a bargain.
SYBIL. Did you?
JESSIE. What's his name? I'd love to meet him.

(*Before VIOLET – obviously caught out – can reply, GILBERT enters from the wings, starting the rehearsal.*)

GILBERT. Beginners, please! On the double!

[MUSIC CUE #3: ORCHESTRA TUNING]

SYBIL. Morning.
JESSIE. Morning!
ROSINA. Good morning!
GILBERT. Clear the stage!
SYBIL. Oh ... here. (*She hands the newspaper to ROSINA, at a loss for what else to do with it.*)
GILBERT. Places! Let's go!

(*The singers take their positions for the opening medley – except ROSINA, who remains center stage, peering at her picture in the "Times." GILBERT is about to cue the number when he sees her.*)

GILBERT. (*With annoyance.*) Rosina ...
ROSINA. Twenty years, and I get my backside in the *Times*.

(*She tosses the paper away and gets into position. GILBERT sighs, all tension.*)

GILBERT. Jessie?!
JESSIE. Ready!
GILBERT. Lights!

[MUSIC CUE #4: MEDLEY]

*(The lights change, and the orchestra begins the
introduction to the opening medley. The medley
consists of excerpts from six Gilbert and Sullivan
hits: "I Have a Song to Sing, O!" from The Yeomen of
the Guard; "Here's a How-de-do" from The Mikado;
"Sad is That Woman's Lot" from Patience; "I'm
Sailing O'er Life's Ocean Wide" from Ruddigore;
"Poor Wand'ring One" from The Pirates of
Penzance; and "Dance a Cachucha" from The
Gondoliers.*

*All the Savoyards [with the exception of GROSSMITH,
who hasn't appeared yet] take part in the medley.
Their roles and solos are indicated below, and they
all join in for the choruses. The medley should be
choreographed so that each number feels special – a
highlight from a past production – yet flows into the
next so that the medley forms an exciting whole. In
particular, the final excerpt, "Dance a Cachucha,"
should be filled with high spirits and tremendous
sound.*

*Also, throughout the medley, GILBERT is scrutinizing
every sound and move. Whenever necessary, he
pushes the singers into better positions and dances
along to show them how to do it. He also calls out
commands, as indicated in the text.)*

<u>SONG TO SING</u>

SYBIL. (Elsie.)
I HAVE A SONG TO SING, O!
   DURWARD. (Point.)
SING ME YOUR SONG, O!
   SYBIL. (Elsie.)
IT IS SUNG WITH A SIGH,
AND A TEAR IN THE EYE,
FOR IT TELLS OF A RIGHT-ED WRONG, O!

IT'S A SONG OF A MERRY MAID, ONCE SO GAY,
WHO TURNED ON HER HEEL AND TRIPPED
   AWAY,
   GILBERT. Good!
   SYBIL. (Elsie.)
FROM THE PEACOCK POPINJAY, BRAVELY BORN,
WHO TURNED UP HIS NOBLE NOSE WITH SCORN
AT THE HUMBLE HEART THAT DID NOT PRIZE;
SO SHE BEGGED ON HER KNEES WITH DOWNCAST
   EYES
FOR THE LOVE OF THE MERRY MAN, MOPING
   MUM,
WHOSE SOUL WAS SAD AND WHOSE GLANCE WAS
   GLUM,
WHO SIPPED NO SUP, AND WHO CRAVED NO
   CRUMB,
AS HE SIGHED FOR THE LOVE OF A LA-DY!
   CHORUS.
HEIGH-DY! HEIGH-DY!
MISERY ME, LACK A DAY-DY!
HIS PAINS WERE O'ER, AND HE SIGHED NO MORE,
FOR HE LIVED IN THE LOVE OF A LA-DY!

HERE'S A HOW-DE-DO

   VIOLET. (Yum Yum.)
HERE'S A HOW-DE-DO!
   COURTICE. (Nanki.)
HERE'S A HOW-DE-DO!
   RUTLAND. (Koko.)
HERE'S A HOW-DE-DO!
   GILBERT. Lighter, lighter.
   VIOLET, COURTICE, RUTLAND.
FOR IF WHAT HE SAYS IS TRUE
I CANNOT, CANNOT MARRY YOU!
HERE'S A PRETTY, PRETTY STATE OF THINGS!

SAD IS THAT WOMAN'S LOT

GILBERT. Turn in pairs!
ROSINA. (Jane.)
SAD IS THAT WOMAN'S LOT WHO, YEAR BY YEAR,
SEES, ONE BY ONE, HER BEAUTIES DISAPPEAR;
    GILBERT. Mirror lower!
    ROSINA. (Jane.)
COMPELLED, AT LAST, IN LIFE'S UNCERTAIN
    GLOAMING
TO WREATHE HER WRINKLED BROW WITH
    WELL SAVED "COMBINGS,"
REDUCED, WITH ROUGE, LIP-SALVE, AND PEARLY
    GREY,
TO "MAKE-UP" FOR LOST TIME AS BEST SHE MAY!

IN SAILING O'ER LIFE'S OCEAN WIDE

JESSIE. (Rose.)

**COURTICE,
DURWARD.** (Richard,
Robin.)

IN SAILING O'ER
LIFE'S OCEAN
WIDE
NO DOUBT THE
HEART SHOULD
BE YOUR GUIDE,
BUT IT IS AWK-
WARD WHEN
YOU FIND
A HEART, A HEART
THAT DOES NOT
KNOW ITS MIND.
A HEART,

A HEART,

IN SAILING O'ER
LIFE'S OCEAN
WIDE
NO DOUBT THE
HEART SHOULD
BE YOUR GUIDE,
BUT IT IS AWK-
WARD WHEN
YOU FIND
A HEART, A HEART
THAT DOES NOT
KNOW ITS MIND.
A HEART THAT
DOES NOT KNOW
ITS MIND
A HEART,

A HEART THAT DOES NOT KNOW ITS MIND	A HEART THAT DOES NOT KNOW ITS MIND
A HEART,	A HEART,
A HEART THAT DOES NOT KNOW ITS MIND!	A HEART THAT DOES NOT KNOW ITS MIND!

POOR WANDERING ONE

VIOLET. (Mabel.)
POOR WAND'RING ONE,
THOUGH THOU HAS SURELY STRAY'D,
TAKE HEART OF GRACE,
THY STEPS RE-TRACE
POOR WANDERING ONE!
   CHORUS.
POOR WANDERING ONE!
   VIOLET. (Mabel.)
AH, AH! AH, AH, AH!
   CHORUS.
POOR WANDERING ONE!
   VIOLET. (Mabel.)
AH, AH! AH, AH, AH!

VIOLET. (Mabel.)	**CHORUS.**
FAIR DAYS WILL SHINE	TAKE HEART
TAKE HEART	TAKE HEART

DANCE A CACHUCHA

ALL.
DANCE A CACHUCHA, FANDANGO, BOLERO,
XERES WE'LL DRINK
MANZANILLA, MONTERO –
WINE, WHEN IT RUNS IN ABUNDANCE,
ENHANCES,

THE RECKLESS DELIGHT OF THAT WILDEST OF
DANCES!
WOMEN.
TO THE PRETTY, PITTER, PITTER, PATTER,
AND THE CLITTER, CLITTER, CLITTER,
CLATTER–
CLITTER, CLITTER, CLATTER,
PITTER, PITTER, PATTER,
CLITTER, CLITTER, CLATTER,
CLITTER, CLITTER, CLATTER –
MEN.
TO THE PRETTY, PITTER, PITTER, PATTER
AND THE CLITTER, CLITTER, CLITTER, CLATTER,
WOMEN.
PITTER, PITTER, PITTER
PATTER, PATTER, PATTER, PATTER WE'LL
DANCE.
ALL.
OLD XERES WE'LL DRINK
MANZANILLA, MONTERO
FOR WINE, WHEN IT RUNS IN ABUNDANCE,
ENHANCES,
THE RECKLESS DELIGHT OF THAT WILDEST OF
DANCES,
THAT WILDEST OF DANCES,
THE RECKLESS DELIGHT!
ALL.
DANCE A CACHUCHA, FANDANGO, BOLERO,
XERES WE'LL DRINK
MANZANILLA, MONTERO –
WINE, WHEN IT RUNS IN ABUNDANCE,
ENHANCES,
THE RECKLESS DELIGHT OF THAT WILDEST OF
DANCES,
OLD XERES WE'LL DRINK
MANZILLA, MONTERO
FOR WINE, WHEN IT RUNS IN ABUNDANCE,
ENHANCES,

THE RECKLESS DELIGHT OF THAT WILDEST OF
    DANCES,
THE RECKLESS DELIGHT OF THAT WILDEST OF
    DANCES,

(*Dance break.*)

ALL.
OLD XERES WE'LL DRINK
MANZANILLA, MONTERO
FOR WINE, WHEN IT RUNS IN ABUNDANCE,
ENHANCES,
THE RECKLESS DELIGHT OF THAT WILDEST OF
    DANCES,
THAT WILDEST OF DANCES.

(*The number at an end, the lights changes and the
singers wait for GILBERT's critique.*)

    GILBERT. Not bad, not bad. A little mushy at the end.
(*To VIOLET.*) Very nice, my dear. Keep it up.
    VIOLET. Thank you.

(*JESSIE and SYBIL stare at each other.*)

    GILBERT. Rutland.
    RUTLAND. Yes sir?
    GILBERT. Do you have fleas, Rutland?
    RUTLAND. Fleas, sir?
    GILBERT. (*Scratching himself.*) Fleas.
    RUTLAND. No sir.
    GILBERT. You were fidgeting on Durward's solo. If
you fidget, they won't listen to him.
    RUTLAND. (*Aside.*) Pity.
    GILBERT. Excuse me?
    RUTLAND. Pretty. Durward's solo, very pretty.
    DURWARD. Thank you so much.

GILBERT. Jessie. (*JESSIE is whispering with SYBIL and doesn't hear him.*) Jessie? ... *Jessie!*

JESSIE. (*Caught.*) Yes. Sorry.

GILBERT. You were screaming.

JESSIE. I wasn't!

GILBERT. Don't tell me you weren't screaming. Shall we take a vote?

SYBIL. (*Raising her hand.*) She was screaming.

GILBERT. So were you!

SYBIL. I was not!

GILBERT. When you scream, I can't hear the words. And the words are very important, aren't they?

THE SINGERS. (*Murmurs.*) Yes sir ... Indeed ...

GILBERT. Crucial.

THE SINGERS. (*Murmurs.*) Crucial ... Mm ...

GILBERT. Next number. That's all the gentlemen. Ladies, please stay out of trouble. If that's possible.

(*The SINGERS disperse. VIOLET exits.*)

GILBERT. Courtice!

COURTICE. (*Entering at a run.*) Right here!

JESSIE. (*To COURTICE.*) Now you shouldn't run, darling. It's bad for the wind. Remember?

COURTICE. Jealous. (*He joins RUTLAND and DURWARD at the wardrobe wagon.*)

SYBIL. Jealous?

JESSIE. That's it. He knows. I'm racked with jealousy.

SYBIL. Oh you poor thing.

JESSIE. If he'd only make love to me. Mad, passionate love. Oh Courtice!

SYBIL. Forget it, dear. He's a tenor. Missing parts, you know.

(*They shriek with laughter.*)

GILBERT. Girls!

JESSIE. Sorry!
SYBIL. Sorry!

(They exit.)

GILBERT. Rutland?
RUTLAND. All set.

(RUTLAND, DURWARD and COURTICE turn, and we see for the first time that they have donned flowing wigs and full-length academic gowns.)

GILBERT. Lights!

(The lights change and the singers assume their poses for "I Am a Maiden Cold and Stately" from Princess Ida. COURTICE, DURWARD and RUTLAND play Hilarion, Cyril and Florian, respectively. The excerpt begins with a short spoken introduction.)

COURTICE. (Hilarion.) But what are these?
RUTLAND. (Florian.) Why, Academic robes, worn by the lady undergraduates.
GILBERT. Words! Words!
RUTLAND. (Florian.) Egad! And now — To storm the castle of our maidens fair, And snatch sweet vict'ry from dark despair.
DURWARD. (Cyril.) We three shall pose and play the parts,
COURTICE. (Hilarion.) Of lovely ladies with three broken hearts!

[MUSIC CUE #6A/B: I AM A MAIDEN COLD AND STATELY]

COURTICE. (Hilarion.)
I AM A MAIDEN, COLD AND STATELY,
HEARTLESS I, WITH A FACE DIVINE.

WHAT DO I WANT WITH A HEART, INNATELY?
EVERY HEART I MEET IS MINE!

(*Just after the song begins, CARTE enters, clipboard in
    hand, and approaches GILBERT. He hates to
    interrupt, but checks his watch and then plunges
    ahead after the first verse.*)

> **CARTE.** William ...
> **GILBERT.** Shh!
> **CARTE.** (*A whisper.*) William ...
> **GILBERT.** Be quiet!

(*Ignored by GILBERT, CARTE once again consults his
    watch, shrugs, then raises his head to the balcony and
    shouts* –)

CARTE. PRIMROSE!? LET'S DO IT! ONE AND
TWO!

(*Immediately the stage is plunged into darkness, except
    for two pin spots shining on CARTE.*)

CARTE. ALL RIGHT! THREE AND FOUR!

(*The lights on CARTE go out, and two more spots come on,
    both on GILBERT, who is glaring murderously. All
    of this happens very quickly.*)

GILBERT. (*Roaring.*) CARTE! Dammit! LIGHTS!

(*The music grinds to a halt as the lights flash back on.*)

> **GILBERT.** Are you mad?! What's the matter with
you?!
> **CARTE.** Ten-fifteen, William. It's on the schedule.
"Lights, check. Singers, break." See? (*He shows him the
schedule.*)

GILBERT. We're running late. Check them later, you idiot.

CARTE. Can't. We may have to order some new bulbs. That's the problem with electricity. Very flashy, but a pain in the –

GILBERT. Carte! Will you get out of here! Now!

CARTE. William, I am in no mood to be trifled with! Durward forgot his music so I had to send someone to Marylebone, Jessie's Venetian costume ripped, and Arthur hasn't even arrived yet!

GILBERT. (*Sarcastically.*) Now that's a surprise.

CARTE. Listen, William. He is just starting to feel better. So don't antagonize him.

GILBERT. Antagonize him? (*Antagonistically.*) I don't antagonize anybody!!

CARTE. William –

GILBERT. Get out of here this instant!

CARTE. (*Definitively.*) William, it is on the schedule!

(*GILBERT pulls out a pencil, takes the schedule board from CARTE and scratches across it vigorously and with obvious pleasure.*)

GILBERT. Not anymore.

CARTE. (*Horrified.*) William. ... I'm the producer!

GILBERT. And just imagine what you could be if you had some talent. (*He turns away.*) Gentlemen, second verse, please. Lights!

(*The song begins again, and CARTE gives up. Throughout the song he busies himself by examining the scenery for signs of wear, rechecking his schedule, etc. As the song continues, his impatience increases.*)

DURWARD. (Cyril.)
I AM A MAIDEN FRANK AND SIMPLE,

BRIMMING WITH JOYOUS ROGUERY;
MERRIMENT LURKS IN EVERY DIMPLE,
NOBODY BREAKS MORE HEARTS THAN I!
    ALL.
HAUGHTY, HUMBLE, COY, OR FREE,
LITTLE CARE I WHAT MAID MAY BE.
SO THAT A MAID IS FAIR TO SEE,
EVERY MAID IS THE MAID FOR ME!
    RUTLAND. (Florian.)
I AM A MAIDEN COYLY BLUSHING,
TIMID AM I AS A STARTLED HIND;
EVERY SUITOR SETS ME FLUSHING;
I AM THE MAID THAT WINS MANKIND!
    ALL.
HAUGHTY, HUMBLE, COY, OR FREE,
LITTLE CARE I WHAT MAID MAY BE.
SO THAT A MAID IS FAIR TO SEE,
EVERY MAID IS THE MAID FOR ME!
    GILBERT. (*On the last note.*) Hold the pose! (*He throws his arms up into the singers' pose.*)
    CARTE. (*Simultaneously.*) REDS UP!

(*The stage instantly turns bright red, freezing GILBERT and the singers into a fiery tableau.*)

    GILBERT. CAAARTE!

Scene 2

A corridor backstage. Immediately following.
A hollow, backstage corridor with a door at one side that leads to Gilbert and Sullivan's dressing room. As the lights come up. SULLIVAN and ALFRED, DUKE OF EDINBURGH enter together. ALFRED, mid-thirties, is an attractive, likeable fellow, filled with nervous

energy. SULLIVAN carries the musical score to "Ivanhoe" under his arm.

ALFRED. Oh I'm so excited. I simply can't thank you enough, Arthur.

SULLIVAN. Don't be silly. It's our pleasure.

ALFRED. It's going to be such fun. I can feel it already. I do hope I'll be all right ...

SULLIVAN. Alfred. You'll be fine. Trust me.

ALFRED. I hope so —

(At this moment, GEORGE GROSSMITH enters with VIOLET. GEORGE is the comic baritone of the company, a dandy, and confident in the extreme. He's in street clothes, his hat set at a jaunty angle.)

GEORGE. Arthur! Welcome!

SULLIVAN. George! How nice to see you. You look well.

GEORGE. I know, I know.

ALFRED. Hello.

SULLIVAN. Ah, now let me present His Royal Highness, the Duke of Edinburgh. Mr. George Grossmith.

GEORGE. Your Royal Highness.

ALFRED. George Grossmith. I've seen you a hundred times. You're simply wonderful!

GEORGE. Well thank you.

SULLIVAN. And, uh ... *(To VIOLET.)* I'm afraid we haven't met.

GEORGE. Oh, sorry. Miss Violet Russell. Our new soprano.

VIOLET. Your Royal Highness.

ALFRED. Pleasure.

GEORGE. Sir Arthur Sullivan.

VIOLET. How do you do.

SULLIVAN. Nice to meet you. Gilbert tells me you sing like an angel.

VIOLET. Thank you.

ALFRED. Seems hardly fair, does it. Talent *and* looks, eh?

GEORGE. Well, I do my best ...

ALFRED. Hm? Oh. Ha! That's good, that's very good!

CARTE. (*Enters.*) Arthur! There you are.

SULLIVAN. Hello, Richard. Sorry I'm late. You know His Royal Highness. Mr. D'Oyly Carte —

CARTE. Of course.

ALFRED. Greetings!

SULLIVAN. Richard, His Royal Highness will be joining us for tonight's performance.

CARTE. How very kind —

SULLIVAN. Singing, I mean. In the show. With the cast.

CARTE. (*Pause.*) What?

GEORGE. Aha.

ALFRED. I can't wait!

SULLIVAN. We've talked about it for years, actually, and we thought tonight, with the Queen coming — his mother ...

ALFRED. She'll be shocked.

CARTE. Yes, I'm sure.

ALFRED. I hope you don't mind.

CARTE. No, no ...

GEORGE. Of course not.

SULLIVAN. George, perhaps you could show his Royal Highness to his dressing room. I thought he might share with you. (*To CARTE.*) Is that all right?

CARTE. (*Grinding his teeth.*) Absolutely, splendid.

GEORGE. Roomies, eh?

ALFRED. That's wonderful.

SULLIVAN. George — ?

GEORGE. Of course. This way ...

ALFRED. Miss Russell, we'll meet again, hm?

VIOLET. I look forward to it.

ALFRED. Au revoir. (*He kisses her hand; then exits, preceding GEORGE down the hall.*) Backstage, eh? Very ... theatrical.

(*GEORGE gives CARTE a look and follows ALFRED. CARTE hangs back.*)

CARTE. (*Aside to SULLIVAN.*) Have you talked to Gilbert about this?
SULLIVAN. I will. I will.
CARTE. Arthur –
SULLIVAN. I promise.
CARTE. Soon! (*Exits.*)

(*SULLIVAN and VIOLET are alone now. SULLIVAN smiles at her cordially. Pause.*)

SULLIVAN. Miss ... Russell, is it?
VIOLET. Yes. Violet.
SULLIVAN. Violet. (*Pause. He glances around. Then –*) You realize, of course, that I shall love you until the day I die.
VIOLET. (*Laughing.*) Oh, Arthur! (*They embrace.*) I never knew you were such an actor!
SULLIVAN. (*Delighted.*) Neither did I! We had them fooled completely. Even Grossmith!
VIOLET. You're such a devil!
SULLIVAN. What I wanted to say was: "George, I already know Miss Russell, thank you, and I adore every inch of her."
VIOLET. Arthur! ... Now we've got to be careful.
SULLIVAN. Absolutely.
VIOLET. You promised me.
SULLIVAN. All right, all right.
VIOLET. Now I'd better go –
SULLIVAN. Wait. What do you say if tonight –
VIOLET. No.
SULLIVAN. Wait –

VIOLET. Not yet.

SULLIVAN. May I finish?! ... If tonight, we don't say anything. We just happen to arrive at the party together.

VIOLET. You don't think they'll guess?

SULLIVAN. So what if they do?

VIOLET. (*Musing.*) I suppose you'll have a lot of people there ...?

SULLIVAN. Everybody. Including the Prince of Wales if we're lucky.

VIOLET. Will he be there?

SULLIVAN. (*Remembering the guest list.*) And the princess, of course. And the Duke of Argyll and Princess Louise ...

VIOLET. (*Breathless.*) O, Arthur – !

SULLIVAN. (*Noticing; amused.*) Good heavens. What a little snob you are.

VIOLET. I'm not –

SULLIVAN. (*Laughing.*) I had no idea –

VIOLET. I'm not!

SULLIVAN. Now what do you say? Hm?

VIOLET. (*Hesitates.*) I don't think so.

SULLIVAN. And the Duke of Connaught, and Lady Brooke, and the Countess of Dudley ... and ... and Lily Langtry!

VIOLET. (*Overlapping and laughing.*) Arthur ... No, no! ... Please. I need more time.

SULLIVAN. I don't know what we're waiting for.

VIOLET. It's my first night! And it's all happened so quickly. My head is spinning. And ... and I want you to know me better. Everything about me.

SULLIVAN. (*Quietly.*) You have very blue eyes, and very blond hair. And when I'm with you, I feel that nothing else in the world matters.

VIOLET. (*Pause. Gently.*) Arthur. Please. At least let's wait for *Ivanhoe.* Till after it opens. You'll be so proud of me then.

SULLIVAN. I'm proud of you now.

VIOLET. You can pick anyone, you know. I won't be hurt.

SULLIVAN. There's no one else in the world who can sing it. I wrote it all for you. Even the baritone. (*They laugh.*) And if you want to wait, we'll wait.

VIOLET. Thank you. Now I must go, really. I've got to rehearse.

SULLIVAN. You are perfect already.

VIOLET. I am not! (*Indicating the door –*) Why don't you take a nap. You look tired.

SULLIVAN. Nonsense.

VIOLET. Go on.

SULLIVAN. I feel fine!

VIOLET. Go on!

(*SULLIVAN sighs and opens the door – pleased to be taken care of. A last smile – then he exits through the door, closing it behind him.*

VIOLET stares at the door for a moment, sighs, then turns to head upstage. Immediately she sees GILBERT, hobbling down the corridor in her direction. She turns and hurries downstage, afraid of being caught –)

GILBERT. Miss Russell. How are you, my dear?

VIOLET. All right.

GILBERT. A little nervous.

VIOLET. I guess so.

GILBERT. Of course you are. And you'll be splendid because of it.

VIOLET. I hope so.

GILBERT. Just remember, my dear, what I tell all of my leading ladies on opening night.

VIOLET. Yes?

GILBERT. (*Philosophically.*) Throughout the performance, Violet, always keep your bosoms parallel to the floor.

VIOLET. (*Straightening up.*) Oh –

GILBERT. No use singing to your feet. They can't hear you.

VIOLET. (*Doubtfully.*) I see ...

GILBERT. You'll be fine.

VIOLET. Thank you. (*Starts to go.*)

GILBERT. Violet ... (*GILBERT looks at her – scrutinizes her – with curiosity.*) Could it have been New York? Last year?

VIOLET. (*Nervously.*) I don't think so. I've never been there.

GILBERT. But we did meet – somewhere? Or I saw you ...?

VIOLET. Oh, if we'd met, I'd remember it. I had a lead once in Melbourne, Australia. Have you been there?

GILBERT. (*Thoughtfully.*) No ...

VIOLET. I was brought up in Adelaide. This is my first time in London.

GILBERT. I see.

VIOLET. But I'm staying. For good, I hope. Unless I make a fool of myself.

GILBERT. Nonsense. Run along now. Ten minutes.

VIOLET. Yes sir.

[MUSIC CUE #7: TRANSITION TO SCENE 3]

(*As she hurries off, GILBERT looks after her, still puzzled. Finally he shrugs, turns and enters the dressing room.*)

Scene 3

Gilbert and Sullivan's dressing room. Immediately following.
Two easy chairs, one with an ottoman for Gilbert's gouty leg, a desk, liquor table [now set for tea], theatrical

posters – the room is a tribute to Victorian masculinity.
SULLIVAN is drowsing in his chair. At the sound of GILBERT'S entrance, SULLIVAN is awakened from his reverie.

SULLIVAN. Hello? ... (*Standing.*) Gilbert!
GILBERT. Sullivan!
SULLIVAN. (*Warmly.*) How are you, old man?
GILBERT. All right, all right. How are you? That's the question?

(*They scrutinize each other.*)

SULLIVAN. Good. Surviving.
GILBERT. You look all right.
SULLIVAN. Surviving. Now sit down with that gout of yours. You need a cup of tea.
GILBERT. (*Pottering to his chair.*) The way I hobble around, what I need is a rickshaw.

(*SULLIVAN goes to the liquor table to pour the tea.*)

SULLIVAN. So how does it look? The show. Are we ready?
GILBERT. (*Sitting.*) Yes, yes. Chorus yesterday, all set. Principals today.
SULLIVAN. How's Rosina?
GILBERT. Enormous.
SULLIVAN. Jessie?
GILBERT. Cheeky.
SULLIVAN. And that uh ... new girl Soprano ...
GILBERT. Violet.
SULLIVAN. Violet. Yes. I just met her, actually, as I was coming in. She's very pretty.
GILBERT. Mm.
SULLIVAN. Extremely beautiful, I'd say.

GILBERT. (*Taking his cup.*) Yes yes yes. Now – who's the girl?

SULLIVAN. Hm?

GILBERT. Miss Wonderful. Now let's go, man to man. Who is she?

SULLIVAN. Gilbert, I can't tell you. I wish I could.

GILBERT. I'll bet.

SULLIVAN. I do. I really do. But she wants to keep it – private for now.

GILBERT. She sounds like trouble.

SULLIVAN. Don't say that! She's an angel.

GILBERT. (*A new tack.*) All right, you can't tell me. Fine. Now listen – last night (– *he takes a piece of paper from his pocket* –) I wrote down several names, which I am going to read aloud –

SULLIVAN. Gilbert –

GILBERT. – and you needn't say a word. You will not *tell* me. However, I shall watch your face.

SULLIVAN. Oh, for heaven's sake!

GILBERT. Maude Reilly.

(*SULLIVAN turns away.*)

GILBERT. This way please.

(*SULLIVAN turns to him, stony.*)

GILBERT. Harriet Fleming.

SULLIVAN. Gilbert, she's married.

GILBERT. I know. That's my theory. Rita Lane.

SULLIVAN. I've never even heard of her.

GILBERT. Little fat thing with a limp.

SULLIVAN. Thanks a lot –

GILBERT. Clarissa Carpenter.

SULLIVAN. Gilbert, stop it! I will not tell you! Just trust me. You'll be the first to know. I promise.

GILBERT. (*Coldly.*) Don't bother. I have just lost interest. I shall not ask you again.

SULLIVAN. Thank you.

(Pause. GILBERT, ignoring SULLIVAN, takes a cigar from a box on the table next to him.)

GILBERT. I still say it's Helen Locksley.
SULLIVAN. Well it isn't.
GILBERT. Yes it is.
SULLIVAN. *(Jumping up.)* It is *not Helen Locksley!!*
GILBERT. I *didn't ask!!*
SULLIVAN. For God's sake – !
GILBERT. *(Eyeing him.)* You're not feeling well, are you?
SULLIVAN. I'm fine! Just because I won't tell you.
GILBERT. You're jumpy. You looked peaked.
SULLIVAN. Not at all. I'm much better. I was quite sick. I almost died in Monte Carlo, you know.
GILBERT. Perhaps you shouldn't conduct tonight. If you're not up to it.
SULLIVAN. Don't be silly. I wouldn't miss it. First night, there I am – eleven shows later, same place.
GILBERT. *(Lighting his cigar.)* Twelve.
SULLIVAN. Hm?
GILBERT. Twelve shows.
SULLIVAN. Eleven, I think.
GILBERT. Twelve.
SULLIVAN. I believe it's eleven.
GILBERT. Twelve.
SULLIVAN. *(Dubiously, ticking them off on his fingers.)* Thespis, Trial by Jury, The Sorcerer, Pinafore, Pirates of Penzance, Patience, Iolanthe, Princess Ida, The Mikado – hear, hear – Yeomen of the Guard and Gondoliers. Eleven.
GILBERT. You left out *Ruddigore.*
SULLIVAN. *(Pause.)* I never liked that one.
GILBERT. You did at the time.
SULLIVAN. No, I never did.
GILBERT. You adored it. You laughed your head off.

SULLIVAN. It was a big mistake. Even the title.
GILBERT. You loved the title!
SULLIVAN. The papers tore it to shreds.
GILBERT. The papers are a lot of molly-coddles.
SULLIVAN. Gilbert, admit it. Nobody liked it!
GILBERT. Wrong! *I* liked it!

(*By this time GILBERT is at the liquor table. He's about to refill his cup, when he spies Sullivan's score of "Ivanhoe" on the table.*)

GILBERT. What's this?
SULLIVAN. Oh, that's nothing.
GILBERT. (*Reading the cover.*) *Ivanhoe.* Grand opera rubbish. Did you bring it here to annoy me? I mean expressly — ?
SULLIVAN. Of course not. I thought I might work on it, during the breaks.
GILBERT. "Libretto by Julian Sturgis." (*Snorts.*) Sturgis. A little walking miracle. A man with the brain of a squirrel.
SULLIVAN. I asked you to write it.
GILBERT. (*Reading.*) "Rebecca, Rebecca. Oh my Rebecca. Oh, Rebecca." Clever line. Million laughs.
SULLIVAN. Gilbert, I begged you to write it.
GILBERT. (*With some passion.*) I thought you did it to be nice and that if I said no you'd get Tennyson to do it. The Poet Laureate. Not some little hack.
SULLIVAN. I shall be remembered for *Ivanhoe.* It will be my masterpiece.
GILBERT. Rubbish.
SULLIVAN. I'm tired of writing entertainments, Gilbert. You know I am. All those rhymes. The same rhythms, over and over ...
GILBERT. I'm sorry if I bore you.

(*Awkward pause. Then suddenly SULLIVAN remembers something.*)

SULLIVAN. (*Nervously.*) Gilbert? I've been meaning to talk to you ...

GILBERT. Hm?

SULLIVAN. (*Choosing his words carefully.*) You know, Alfred ... Alfred ...?

GILBERT. Alfie? Yes. Dumbbell with the title.

SULLIVAN. He's been a very good friend to me, as it happens. And he's quite a great fan of yours.

GILBERT. I'll bet.

SULLIVAN. You've never given him a fair chance, you know. Honestly, he's not a bad musician. Not at all. Plays the fiddle.

GILBERT. Really? Which end?

(*SULLIVAN becomes increasingly agitated.*)

SULLIVAN. Now there you go again. I mean, my God, the Queen's son — he is the Queen's son.

GILBERT. She ought to know.

SULLIVAN. And he has influence. For God's sake, the man knows everyone. And everybody knows Alfred. Of course, I realize it's late.

GILBERT. Late?

SULLIVAN. Late. Late in the day.

GILBERT. Late for what? Sullivan, you're not making sense! What are you talking about?!

SULLIVAN. (*Carefully.*) Gilbert ... Alfred has asked me time and again if he might appear in one of our shows. Briefly.

GILBERT. Hah!

SULLIVAN. And I have always dissuaded him. But — this time ... I think we should reconsider.

GILBERT. (*Stunned.*) Are you mad?

SULLIVAN. William, please. For his mother, the Queen! Don't you see? She'll love it! The audience will love it. It's a revue!

GILBERT. Ha!

SULLIVAN. One song. One little song. Just for tonight! What do you say?

GILBERT. You're out of your mind.

SULLIVAN. Gilbert, listen to me! Just *listen* - !

GILBERT. (*Suddenly realizing.*) You said yes, didn't you? Already. Without asking me!

SULLIVAN. No! Of course not! ... Not exactly.

GILBERT. What does that mean? "Not exactly"?

SULLIVAN. Not exactly! What do you think it means?! It means *not exactly!*

(*A knock at the door. SULLIVAN freezes.*)

SULLIVAN. (*Weakly.*) Yes?

ALFRED. (*Off, cheerfully.*) Alfred!

SULLIVAN. Just a minute! (*Sotto voce.*) Gilbert, for God's sake it won't kill you. Just one song, a little dancing −

GILBERT. Dancing?!

SULLIVAN. Gilbert −

GILBERT. Open the door.

SULLIVAN. No, wait. We have two votes. And I vote yes.

GILBERT. (*In high dudgeon.*) Open the *door.*

(*SULLIVAN goes to the door and opens it. ALFRED springs into the room in full pirate costume − bandanna, cutlass, eyepatch, the works.*)

ALFRED. "Ohhhhh! I polished up the handle so carefulee, That now I am the ruler of the Queen's Navee!" So what do you think?!

GILBERT. (*Pause.*) I think your mother will be very proud. (*SULLIVAN and GILBERT look at each other. The scene changes.*)

[MUSIC CUE #7B: BRIDGE TO SCENE 4]

Scene 4

The Savoy stage. A half hour later.

[MUSIC CUE #8: LYING AWAKE]

As the scene changes, the orchestra begins a sly and haunting canon – the introduction to "When You're Lying Awake" from "Iolanthe." Then a spotlight comes up on GEORGE, standing alone onstage in the costume of the Lord Chancellor.

RECITATIVE

GEORGE. (Lord Chancellor.)
LOVE, UNREQUITED, ROBS ME OF MY REST:
LOVE, HOPELESS LOVE, MY ARDENT SOUL ENCUMBERS:
LOVE, NIGHTMARE-LIKE, LIES HEAVY ON MY CHEST,
AND WEAVES ITSELF INTO MY MIDNIGHT SLUMBERS!

SONG

WHEN YOU'RE LYING AWAKE WITH A DISMAL HEADACHE, AND REPOSE IS TABOO'D BY ANXIETY,
I CONCEIVE YOU MAY USE ANY LANGUAGE YOU CHOOSE TO INDULGE IN, WITHOUT IMPROPRIETY;
FOR YOUR BRAIN IS ON FIRE – THE BEDCLOTHES CONSPIRE OF USUAL SLUMBER TO PLUNDER YOU:
FIRST YOUR COUNTERPANE GOES, AND UNCOVERS YOUR TOES, AND YOUR SHEET SLIPS DEMURELY FROM UNDER YOU;

THEN THE BLANKETING TICKLES – YOU FEEL
LIKE MIXED PICKLES – SO TERRIBLY SHARP IS
THE PRICKING,
AND YOU'RE HOT, AND YOU'RE CROSS, AND YOU
TUMBLE AND TOSS TILL THERE'S NOTHING
'TWIXT YOU AND THE TICKING.
THEN THE BEDCLOTHES ALL CREEP TO THE
GROUND IN A HEAP, AND YOU PICK 'EM ALL UP
IN A TANGLE;
NEXT YOUR PILLOW RESIGNS AND POLITELY
DECLINES TO REMAIN AT ITS USUAL ANGLE!
WELL, YOU GET SOME REPOSE IN THE FORM OF A
DOZE, WITH HOT EYE-BALLS AND HEAD EVER
ACHING,
BUT YOUR SLUMBERING TEEMS WITH SUCH
HORRIBLE DREAMS THAT YOU'D VERY MUCH
BETTER BE WAKING;
FOR YOU DREAM YOU ARE CROSSING THE
CHANNEL, AND TOSSING ABOUT IN A
STEAMER FROM HARWICH –
WHICH IS SOMETHING BETWEEN A LARGE
BATHING MACHINE AND A VERY SMALL
SECOND-CLASS CARRIAGE –
AND YOU'RE GIVING A TREAT (PENNY ICE AND
COLD MEAT) TO A PARTY OF FRIENDS AND
RELATIONS –
THEY'RE A RAVENOUS HORDE – AND THEY ALL
CAME ON BOARD AT SLOANE SQUARE AND
SOUTH KENSINGTON STATIONS.
AND BOUND ON THAT JOURNEY YOU FIND YOUR
ATTORNEY (WHO STARTED THAT MORNING
FROM DEVON);
HE'S A BIT UNDERSIZED, AND YOU DON'T FEEL
SURPRISED WHEN HE TELLS YOU HE'S ONLY
ELEVEN.
WELL YOU'RE DRIVING LIKE MAD WITH THIS
SINGULAR LAD (BY THE BY, THE SHIP'S NOW A
FOUR-WHEELER),

AND YOU'RE PLAYING ROUND GAMES, AND HE
CALLS YOU BAD NAMES WHEN YOU TELL HIM
THAT "TIES PAY THE DEALER";
BUT THIS YOU CAN'T STAND, SO YOU THROW UP
YOUR HAND, AND YOU FIND YOU'RE AS COLD
AS AN ICICLE,
IN YOUR SHIRT AND YOUR SOCKS (THE BLACK
SILK WITH GOLD CLOCKS), CROSSING
SALISBURY PLAIN ON A BICYCLE:
AND HE AND THE CREW ARE ON BICYCLES TOO –
WHICH THEY'VE SOMEHOW OR OTHER
INVESTED IN –
AND HE'S TELLING THE TARS ALL THE
PARTIC U*LARS* OF A COMPANY HE'S
INTERESTED IN –
IT'S A SCHEME OF DEVICES, TO GET AT LOW
PRICES ALL GOODS FROM COUGH MIXTURES
TO CABLES
(WHICH TICKLED THE SAILORS), BY TREATING
RETAILERS AS THOUGH THEY WERE ALL
VEG*T*ABLES –
YOU GET A GOOD SPADESMAN TO PLANT A SMALL
TRADESMAN (FIRST TAKE OFF HIS BOOTS
WITH A BOOT-TREE),
AND HIS LEGS WILL TAKE ROOT, AND HIS
FINGERS WILL SHOOT, AND THEY'LL
BLOSSOM AND BUD LIKE A FRUIT-TREE –
FROM THE GREENGROCER TREE YOU GET
GRAPES AND GREEN PEA, CAULIFLOWER,
PINEAPPLE, AND CRANBERRIES,
WHILE THE PASTRY COOK PLANT CHERRY
BRANDY WILL GRANT, APPLE PUFFS, AND
THREE-CORNERS, AND BANBURYS –
THE SHARES ARE A PENNY, AND EVER SO MANY
ARE TAKEN BY ROTHSCHILD AND BARING,
AND JUST AS A FEW ARE ALLOTTED TO YOU, YOU
AWAKE WITH A SHUDDER DESPAIRING

YOU'RE A REGULAR WRECK, WITH A CRICK IN YOUR NECK, AND NO WONDER YOU SNORE, FOR YOUR HEAD'S ON THE FLOOR, AND YOU'VE NEEDLES AND PINS FROM YOUR SOLES TO YOUR SHINS, AND YOUR FLESH IS A-CREEP, FOR YOUR LEFT LEG'S ASLEEP, AND YOU'VE CRAMP IN YOUR TOES, AND A FLY ON YOUR NOSE, AND SOME FLUFF IN YOUR LUNG, AND A FEVERISH TONGUE, AND A THIRST THAT'S INTENSE, AND A GENERAL SENSE THAT YOU HAVEN'T BEEN SLEEPING IN CLOVER;
BUT THE DARKNESS HAS PASSED, AND IT'S DAYLIGHT AT LAST, AND THE NIGHT HAS BEEN LONG – DITTO DITTO MY SONG – AND THANK GOODNESS THEY'RE BOTH OF THEM OVER!

(The LORD CHANCELLOR falls exhausted onto the floor. As the performance lights change to rehearsal lights, we hear ROSINA, offstage. A moment later, she rushes on, dressed as the Queen of the Fairies from "Iolanthe.")

ROSINA. *(Off.)* George! ... *(Entering.)* George! Guess what!
GEORGE. I give up.
ROSINA. Guess who's in the show tonight!
GEORGE. The Duke of Edinburgh.
ROSINA. *(Deflated.)* How did you know?
GEORGE. He's sharing my dressing room.
ROSINA. Oh you lucky stick. He's gorgeous. I could just eat him up.
GEORGE. I'll bet.
ROSINA. Now listen to this! I passed him in the hall just now, and I sort of waved. And then he smiled at me – the most beautiful smile –

(JESSIE and SYBIL enter from the wings, excited, both in costume for "Iolanthe.")

JESSIE. Rosina!
SYBIL. Guess what!
JESSIE. Just guess!
ROSINA. I know, I know! Isn't he wonderful!
SYBIL. He's so handsome!
ROSINA. I was just telling George how I met him —
JESSIE. Already?
ROSINA. You see I passed him in the hall, and I sort of waved, and then he smiled at me. So! I walked right up to him, bold as brass —
SYBIL. You didn't!
ROSINA. I did! I walked right up and said "Your Highness?" And he stopped. And then he looked straight at me, with those dreamy eyes, and he said —
GILBERT. *(Entering with CARTE.)* Places! Let's go, let's go!
ROSINA. He looked straight at me, and he said —
CARTE. Places, please! Right away!

(GILBERT and CARTE confer.)

JESSIE. What did he say!?
SYBIL. Hurry up!
ROSINA. I'm telling you — !

(RUTLAND and COURTICE, dressed as peers for "Iolanthe", enter from the wings.)

COURTICE. Hey girls, guess what!
RUTLAND. You'll never guess it in a million years— !
SYBIL. We know!
JESSIE. We know!
SYBIL. Rosina met him.
RUTLAND. No joke.

ROSINA. Just *listen*! In the hall, I waved, he smiled, I said "Your Highness," he looked at me ... and he said "Rosina Brandram, I believe?" Just like that.

SYBIL. Did he really?

CARTE. Rosina!

ROSINA. Coming! ... So I said "You know me?" – I was rather surprised – and he said "I've seen a lot of you onstage."

GEORGE. Well, there's a lot of you to see onstage.

GILBERT. (*An explosion.*) ROSINA!!!

ROSINA. All right, all right. (*Muttering.*) For God's sake ...

(*The cast move into position for the next number.*)

GILBERT. (*Quietly.*) Ladies and gentlemen. We have nine hours until the Queen of England arrives at this theatre. Do you understand that? NINE HOURS!

ROSINA. We're ready, Billy.

GILBERT. Lights!

[MUSIC CUE #9: IOLANTHE MEDLEY]

(*The lights change, and the singers perform an excerpt from "Iolanthe". The excerpt consists of two parts: an introduction composed of a verse from the beginning of Act I and a recitative from the Finale to Act I; and the song "If You Go In" from Act II. GEORGE, RUTLAND and COURTICE play the Lord Chancellor, Mountararat and Tolloller, respectively; and ROSINA, JESSIE and SYBIL play the Queen, Iolanthe and Phyllis, respectively.*
The story of the song focuses on ROSINA, buxom Queen of the Fairies: she offers herself repeated to the shy Lord Chancellor, who at last succumbs to her pressing charms in the final verse.)

<u>VERSE</u>

ROSINA. (Queen.)
WE ARE DAINTY LITTLE FAIRIES, EVER SINGING,
    EVER DANCING;
WE INDULGE IN OUR VAGARIES IN A FASHION
    MOST ENTRANCING.
IF YOU ASK THE SPECIAL FUNCTION OF OUR
    NEVER-CEASING MOTION,
WE REPLY, WITHOUT COMPUNCTION, THAT WE
    HAVEN'T ANY NOTION!
 JESSIE and SYBIL. (Iolanthe and Phyllis.)
NO WE HAVEN'T ANY NOTION,
ANY NOTION!
 GEORGE. (Lord Chancellor.) (*Spoken; convulsed.*)
Ha ha ha! ... No notion! ... They haven't any ... Ha! ...

(*The Queen gives him a look, and he stops abruptly.*)

 ROSINA. (Queen.)
OH! CHANCELLOR UNWARY
IT'S HIGHLY NECESSARY
YOUR TONGUE TO TEACH
RESPECTFUL SPEECH –
YOUR ATTITUDE TO VARY!

YOUR BADINAGE SO AIRY,
YOUR MANNER ARBITRARY,
ARE OUT OF PLACE
WHEN FACE TO FACE
WITH AN INFLUENTIAL FAIRY.
 PEERS.
WE NEVER KNEW
WE WERE TALKING TO
AN INFLUENTIAL FAIRY!
 GEORGE. (Lord Chancellor.)
A PLAGUE ON THIS VAGARY,
I'M IN A NICE QUANDARY!

OF HASTY TONE
WITH DAMES UNKNOWN
I OUGHT TO BE MORE CHARY;
IT SEEMS THAT SHE'S A FAIRY
FROM ANDERSEN'S LIBRARY,
AND I TOOK HER FOR
THE PROPRIETOR
OF A LADIES' SEMINARY!
    PEERS.
WE TOOK HER FOR
THE PROPRIETOR
OF A LADIES' SEMINARY!
    RUTLAND. (Lord Mountararat.)
IF YOU GO IN YOU'RE SURE TO WIN –
YOURS WILL BE THE CHARMING MAIDIE:
BE YOUR LAW
THE ANCIENT SAW,
"FAINT HEART NEVER WON FAIR LADY!"
    GEORGE, RUTLAND, AND COURTICE. (Lord
Chancellor, Mountararat , Tolloller.)
FAINT HEART NEVER WON FAIR LADY!
EVERY JOURNEY HAS AN END –
WHEN AT THE WORST AFFAIRS WILL MEND –
DARK THE DAWN WHEN DAY IS NIGH –
HUSTLE YOUR HORSE AND DON'T SAY DIE!
    ROSINA. (Queen.)
HE WHO SHIES
AT SUCH A PRIZE
IS NOT WORTH A MARAVEDI,
BE SO KIND
TO BEAR IN MIND –
FAINT HEART NEVER WON FAIR LADY!
JESSIE, ROSINA AND SYBIL. (Iolanthe, Queen,
Phyllis.)
FAINT HEART NEVER WON FAIR LADY!
WHILE THE SUN SHINES MAKE YOUR HAY –
WHERE A WILL IS, THERE'S A WAY
BEARD THE LION IN HIS LAIR –

NONE BUT THE BRAVE DESERVE THE FAIR!
   GEORGE. (Lord Chancellor.)
I'LL TAKE HEART
AND MAKE A START
THOUGH I FEAR THE PROSPECT'S SHADY,
MUCH I'D SPEND
TO GAIN MY END
FAINT HEART NEVER WON FAIR LADY!
   ALL MEN.
FAINT HEART NEVER WON FAIR LADY!
NOTHING VENTURE, NOTHING WIN
BLOOD IS THICK, BUT WATER'S THIN
IN FOR A PENNY, IN FOR A POUND
IT'S LOVE THAT MAKES THE WORLD GO ROUND!
   ALL.
NOTHING VENTURE, NOTHING WIN
BLOOD IS THICK, BUT WATER'S THIN
IN FOR A PENNY, IN FOR A POUND
IT'S LOVE THAT MAKES THE WORLD GO ROUND!

[MUSIC CUE #10: BRIDGE TO SCENE 5]

Scene 5

*A dressing room, green room and corridor, backstage.
Immediately following.*
*Three playing areas: Stage right is Violet's dressing
room, small, with an exit upstage to the adjoining
dressing room and an exit left to the green room. The
green room also has two exits, the one to the dressing
room and a door left to the corridor. The corridor can
play in front of the rooms or stage left; in the latter
case, two or three dull lights could hang in a row from
above.*

*Both rooms are cluttered and worn, costumes and hats
   hanging on the walls. The dressing room has at least
   a make-up table and a folding screen in one corner.
   The green room has at least a small sofa. The two
   rooms are essentially a single flat, and the "door"
   that joins them can be a frame with a curtain.*
*When the lights come up, ALFRED and VIOLET are
   sitting next to each other on the sofa having a high old
   time. ALFRED, at the moment, has VIOLET in
   stitches with one of his stories.*

VIOLET. (*Laughing.*) Oh no! ...

ALFRED. Perfectly true, I swear it. Gobs of them. So
then he takes one look at her and he says – mind you, this
is the King of Denmark – he says, "I see that Lady
Richmond is doing her walking chandelier imitation."
Ha! (*He laughs uproariously, as does VIOLET.*) Yes ...
yes ... Oh-h ... I haven't had so much fun since my
brother fell into the cake at a state wedding. Ha! (*They're
off again.*)

(*As they roar with laughter, ROSINA, JESSIE and SYBIL,
   still in costume from "Iolanthe", enter from the
   corridor.*)

ALFRED. (*Jovially; standing.*) Ladies!

ALL THREE. (*Dumfounded.*) Your Royal Highness
... Your Royal Highness ...

ALFRED. Oh stop that. We're all troupers here, eh?
Hm?

ROSINA. (*Heading straight for him, in full sail.*) Oh
absolutely. And it's so lovely to see you again, Your Royal
Highness.

ALFRED. (*Backing off.*) It is indeed.

---

* Alternatively, instead of a green room, the first half of the scene
could be played on a landing outside Violet's dressing room, using
a bench in place of the green room sofa.

ROSINA. I'll make the introductions, shall I? Jessie Bond and Sybil Grey. My very dear friend, His Royal Highness, the Duke of Edinburgh.

JESSIE. Your Royal Highness.

SYBIL. How do you do?

ALFRED. Egad, you're all pretty in this place. Good thing I'm not a regular, eh? I'd wreak havoc.

ROSINA. (*The coquette.*) Would you really ...?

ALFRED. You'd all be in danger.

ROSINA. How very frightening.

ALFRED. Shall I go? Am I in the way – ?

ROSINA. Oh not at all. Please do sit down, Your Royal Highness –

(*She starts to sit, but JESSIE and SYBIL lift her up again –*

SYBIL. Rosina –

JESSIE. We must be going, I'm afraid –

ROSINA. (*Put out.*) Girls ...

SYBIL. Honestly –

JESSIE. Rosina – !

SYBIL. Think of the *lady's side* of things.

ROSINA. Hm? The lady's – ? Oh. Oh of course. (*She stands her ground for a moment.*) Well before I go, I just want to say, that we girls are thrilled to have you aboard, sir. Welcome. (*She extends her hand.*)

ALFRED. Thank you, my dear. (*He kisses her hand.*) Aye aye!

ROSINA. (*Overcome.*) Oh ... (*She floats backward.*)

(*JESSIE and SYBIL pull ROSINA into the dressing room.*)

ROSINA. A bientot!

(*They continue through the door right, and they're gone.*)

ALFRED. (*Pleased.*) What a crew!

VIOLET. Yes.

ALFRED. (*Pause.*) Now what about you, eh? I want to hear everything. Behind the scenes.

VIOLET. There's nothing to tell, I'm afraid.

ALFRED. Well of course there is. Life story, come on. Now when did you start singing? In the crib, I'll bet. Born to the lights. Mother, Sarah Bernhardt.

VIOLET. No.

ALFRED. No? Tsk tsk tsk. Then how'd you do it? Tell me.

VIOLET. I don't know. Luck, I guess. Of course, I knew I could sing, I knew that. And then I ... started at the bottom, actually.

ALFRED. Good for you. I like that.

VIOLET. You do?

ALFRED. Of course I do. Spunk. Singing away at all those church socials ...

VIOLET. (*Carefully.*) No. You don't understand. You see, I always sang for money.

ALFRED. Well, that's excellent. Why not? I have been asked frequently, at parties, *not* to sing for money. Hah! ... And now you want to be famous, right? Jenny Lind.

VIOLET. I ... think so.

ALFRED. You're not sure?

VIOLET. Well I think I'm sure. Sometimes I want to do everything! ... But ... I don't know ... it all seems so complicated, especially when other people get involved, and you can't ignore them, but you have to make the right decision. Except, you never really know if it's right until you've made it, and then it's too late. Does that make any sense?

ALFRED. Not especially, no ... Are you married?

VIOLET. No. Not yet. You are.

ALFRED. Yes. Yes, very much so. Marie of Russia. Daughter of the Tsar. Arranged, you know. Hatched in St. Petersburg. Wonderful woman, really. Very ...

efficient. Taught her a few card games once. Next thing you know, she wiped out my entire club.

VIOLET. I'm terrible at cards.

ALFRED. Are you? So am I. On my old ship, I used to lose deliberately so the mates would like me — now I can't win to save my life.

VIOLET. I'll bet you can.

ALFRED. No. Honestly.

VIOLET. You can.

ALFRED. Not a game. Ever.

VIOLET. Well you could beat me.

ALFRED. You'd kill me.

VIOLET. I wouldn't. I'm terrible.

ALFRED. All right, it's a match. We'll both sit there trying to lose.

VIOLET. (*Laughing.*) All right. If I win, I'll ... I'll buy you a drink. May I?

ALFRED. Absolutely. And if I win, I'll buy you Harrod's.

(*Pause. ALFRED is feeling a little awkward, realizing how well they're getting on.*)

ALFRED. So ...

VIOLET. It's your first time in a play, isn't it?

ALFRED. Mm.

VIOLET. Are you nervous?

ALFRED. Mm.

VIOLET. I thought so.

ALFRED. You did?

VIOLET. Well, I mean you'd have to be. First time ever.

ALFRED. Well it's a funny thing. One minute I know all my lines, bang bang bang, nothing to it, and the next minute it's all gone. You know what I mean?

VIOLET. Yes ...

ALFRED. Mm...

VIOLET. But it's all a trick, you know.

ALFRED. It is?

VIOLET. Really. It's just a matter of concentration. Putting yourself into the character. I mean, don't think of yourself at Alfr ... the Duke of –

ALFRED. Alfred.

VIOLET. All right ... Alfred. But think of that character you're playing and get into him. Think of what he'd say or sing in that situation. You see?

ALFRED. (*Slowly.*) That's good. I like that. That's very good.

VIOLET. It's a matter of thinking all the time.

ALFRED. Thinking. I'll try it. (*Pause. He gazes at her.*) How old are you?

VIOLET. (*Hesitating.*) ... Twenty-three. But I look older.

ALFRED. A good fifty.

VIOLET. Alfred, you embarrass me.

ALFRED. Do I? How wonderful.

VIOLET. Oh, you're so wicked ...

ALFRED. Wicked! Hah ...

(*By this time GILBERT has entered the corridor and knocks on the door left.*)

ALFRED. Entrez!

(*GILBERT enters, and VIOLET rises quickly. GILBERT, seeing ALFRED, stops in his tracks.*)

ALFRED. Gilbert! You're just in time! The girl says I'm wicked. What do you think?

GILBERT. (*Coldly.*) I assume that you know where you are, Your Royal Highness.

ALFRED. (*Bewildered.*) I think so.

GILBERT. This is the ladies' side. Men are not permitted here.

ALFRED. But you're here.

GILBERT. I'm the director!

ALFRED. Oh. Oh! (*He jumps up.*) Sorry. I see –

GILBERT. (*Trying to control himself.*) We have rules, sir.

VIOLET. I'm sorry.

ALFRED. (*Flustered.*) My fault – my fault entirely! I simply pushed my way in – !

GILBERT. (*Overlapping.*) We have a reputation – !

ALFRED. (*Overlapping.*) I wouldn't budge – !

GILBERT. (*Overlapping.*) – with our audience!

ALFRED. Right! I'm just going.

GILBERT. And get into costume!

ALFRED. Right. Costume?

GILBERT. The *Mikado* Medley. You have three minutes.

ALFRED. Oh, I forgot. (*He chuckles nervously.*) Silly me. Costume. I'll be there! (*To VIOLET.*) Good-bye, my dear.

(*He hurries through the door to the dressing room which of course is the wrong way. GILBERT tries to stop him, but it's too late. ALFRED hurries through the room and goes through the door to the adjoining offstage dressing room. Screams and giggles erupt. He immediately runs back through the dressing room and into the green room area.*)

ALFRED. (*Feigning nonchalance.*) Wrong door ... (*He exits quickly down the corridor and disappears.*)

GILBERT. You surprise me, Miss Russell.

VIOLET. I – I'm sorry. I didn't know.

GILBERT. You didn't know?

VIOLET. No, I really didn't.

GILBERT. Well you do now.

VIOLET. Yes sir.

(*GILBERT turns abruptly and exits through the door left, slamming it as he goes. As he marches down the*

*corridor, he shouts "Three minutes, ladies!" — then
disappears.
VIOLET stands alone for a moment, angry at her
carelessness. Then she enters the dressing room,
which is empty. She begins to undress, pulling her
skirt off with obvious annoyance. After a moment,
JESSIE and SYBIL enter from the adjoining dressing
room, in their Mikado costumes.)*

SYBIL. Is he gone?
VIOLET. What do you think?

*(JESSIE   and SYBIL exchange glances as VIOLET
continues to strip.)*

JESSIE. Tsk tsk tsk. Oh dear.
SYBIL. Dear dear dear.
JESSIE. Don't get ruffled, Vi.
VIOLET. You could have told me about the rules.
JESSIE. We thought you knew.
SYBIL. Besides, I thought it was very sweet of you to
entertain him for us. Didn't you, Jess?
JESSIE. Charming.
SYBIL. I wonder ... Do you think he's gone? I mean
really.
JESSIE. Perhaps he's hiding.
SYBIL. That's it. Under the bed.
JESSIE. There is no bed.
SYBIL. No bed? What a waste.
JESSIE. *(Peering into the wardrobe.)* Duke? Your
Highness?
SYBIL. *(And behind the screen.)* Du-uke?
VIOLET. Will you get out, please.
SYBIL. I know ... *(She throws Violet's petticoats up
from behind. Screams –)* Your Highness!
JESSIE. *(Overlapping.)* Oh! Royalty!
VIOLET. *Bitch!* *(She regrets this immediately. A
tense pause.)* I'm sorry. But you're being unfair. You

know that. (*She retreats behind the screen to finish undressing.*)

    SYBIL. Sorry.

    JESSIE. Sorry.

    SYBIL. Just having fun, Vi.

    JESSIE. No offense.

    VIOLET. (*From behind the screen.*) Forget it. (*JESSIE and SYBIL look at each other.*) Would you hand me my costume, please.

    SYBIL. (*Picks up Violet's costume; hesitates.*) Certainly. What costume?

    JESSIE. (*Catching on.*) Costume?

    VIOLET. The kimono

    JESSIE. (*To SYBIL.*) Kimono?

    SYBIL. I don't see a kimono. (*She tosses it to JESSIE, who tosses it back. SYBIL waves it like a matador's cape and JESSIE runs through it like a bull.*)

    VIOLET. The red one. On the chair.

    SYBIL. Red one?

    JESSIE. On the chair?

    SYBIL. (*To JESSIE.*) Do you see it? (*She and JESSIE hurriedly stuff VIOLET's kimono out of sight under the sofa pillow.*)

    JESSIE. I don't see it.

    SYBIL. I did see it.

    JESSIE. Good heavens, it's late. We've got to go.

    SYBIL. Good heavens!

    JESSIE. Good-bye, dear. Hope you find it.

    VIOLET. Jessie ...

    JESSIE. See you onstage.

    SYBIL. (*Switching off the lights.*) Oh dear, the lights!

    JESSIE. Damn that electricity. It's so unreliable.

    SYBIL. Dear dear dear!

(*They run laughing through the door right, closing it behind them, obscuring the room in darkness. As they hurry down the corridor and out of sight they pass*

*GILBERT heading the other way. This and the
following action occur very quickly.*
As *GILBERT continues toward the door, VIOLET
emerges from behind the screen, groping her way in
the darkness. She's barely dressed, in a corset and
knickers.*)

VIOLET. Jessie ... Sybil ... Will you stop it – Ow!
(*She hits her knee on the chair.*) Damn! (*She pushes the
chair aside, knocking it over.*) Damn! (*She finds the door
and flings it open.*) Will ya give me my bloody costume!

(*Directly in front of the door stands GILBERT. For a split
second they both freeze in the bright light of the
corridor, VIOLET half-naked and GILBERT
dumbfounded.*)

GILBERT. Oh my God!

(*VIOLET screams and slams the door.*)

GILBERT. ... I've got it!

(*The scene changes around GILBERT, who stands
immobile, in a daze.*)

[MUSIC CUE #11: BRIDGE TO SCENE 6]

Scene 6

*The Savoy Stage. Immediately following.
The cast are assembling for the "Mikado" medley, and
the growing tension of opening night is getting to
some of them. DURWARD and COURTICE are
arguing about a costume, ROSINA is primping with*

*annoyance, JESSIE and SYBIL are practicing with
their fans, etc. During the following, GILBERT is in
a daze, oblivious to all of them.*

COURTICE. That's my costume!
DURWARD. It is not!
COURTICE. Look at the label.
DURWARD. Well they got it wrong!
ROSINA. I hate this wig. I just hate it!

*(By this time KITTY has entered in her overcoat and hat.
She is looking for GILBERT, but he spots her first.)*

GILBERT. Kitty! (*He hurries over to her.*)
KITTY. William. There you are.
GEORGE. Come here ...
KITTY. I have the notes you wanted.
GILBERT. (*Drawing her aside.*) Come here! Listen!
KITTY. William ...
GILBERT. I know who she is. The girl.
KITTY. What girl?
GILBERT. (*Whispering now.*) Violet Russell. I told
you I recognized her –
KITTY. Did you?
GILBERT. Of course I did! Don't you ever listen to
me?
KITTY. Sometimes, dear.

*(CARTE has entered by this time, inspecting scenery.
GILBERT spots him.)*

GILBERT. Carte! Come here!
CARTE. In a moment.
GILBERT. Now!
KITTY. William ...
GILBERT. (*Pulling CARTE into their little circle.*)
Just listen. Carte, do you remember I said that Violet
looked familiar.

CARTE. Violet?

GILBERT. Violet Russell. Well it just came back. (*Dramatically* –) She was a dancer at the South London Palace!

KITTY & CARTE. So?

GILBERT. The Palace, Carte. She was a ... a .. dancing girl. (*Rolling his shoulders and hips* –) She bent over and ... and ... wiggled. In her knickers. With her bottom!

CARTE. William ...

GILBERT. I saw it. With my own eyes!

KITTY. You did? How very interesting.

GILBERT. Oh Kitty, grow up. We've got a problem.

CARTE. What problem?

GILBERT. Carte, the girl exposed herself! Good Lord, man, imagine if the papers got hold of it. "Queen Meets Dancing-Girl at Command Performance" –

KITTY. "Queen Faints."

CARTE. "Gilbert Faints."

KITTY. "On Top of Her!" (*They laugh.*)

GILBERT. It isn't funny! Now what are we going to do?!

CARTE. Do?

GILBERT. Well she can't go on.

CARTE. Of course she'll go on.

GILBERT. Carte, are you insane – !

CARTE. William! You probably have the wrong girl, number one, and number two, I don't care if she sang *God Save the Queen* on the lawn of Buckingham Palace stark naked! (*To KITTY.*) Sorry. (*To GILBERT.*) She has good ankles, a lovely voice and the show opens in eight hours. Now stay out of it!

GILBERT. Fine. Fine! I will talk to Sullivan.

CARTE. Don't you dare.

GILBERT. But Carte – !

CARTE. That is just the sort of thing to upset him.

KITTY. I agree.

GILBERT. (*To KITTY.*) You keep out of this!

CARTE. Listen, William, and listen carefully. I have spent the better part of a lifetime keeping you two from each other's throats. When you aren't speaking, I carry messages. When you make it up, I play the goat. I have been whacked back and forth so many times I feel like a tennis ball. Now I can smell an argument between you two a mile off, and this time I won't have it. Do you hear me, William, I *will not have it.!!*

GILBERT. Well I don't like it. It's bad enough we have the Duke of Edinburgh prancing around here like an ape off his leash.

CARTE. William, *drop* it. Either you want to do more shows together or you don't. That's all I have to say. (*Walks away.*)

GILBERT. (*Mimicking CARTE.*) That's all I have to say ...

KITTY. Don't pout, dear.

(*As GILBERT stews, SULLIVAN enters from the wings. A buzz of excitement goes through the cast.*)

SYBIL. Sir Arthur.

SULLIVAN. Hello, Sybil ...

JESSIE. (*Warmly.*) Welcome back, Sir Arthur.

SULLIVAN. Thank you, Jessie. Durward, Courtice, Rutland ... Rosina! (*He kisses her hand.*)

ROSINA. Oh, Arthur. You old flirt.

GILBERT. (*In a foul mood.*) All right, all right, come on. Sullivan!

SULLIVAN. Kitty! My dear, how are you? You look wonderful! (*They embrace.*)

KITTY. So do you, Arthur. A sight for sore eyes.

GILBERT. (*To KITTY.*) Good-bye, dear. Thank you for stopping.

KITTY. (*Sighs.*) How do I do it, Arthur?

SULLIVAN. I don't know, my dear.

GILBERT. Sullivan!

SULLIVAN. All right, all right ...

GILBERT. Places!

(KITTY exits as SULLIVAN descends to the pit. Meanwhile, as the cast move into position, ALFRED strides in, dressed colorfully as a Japanese Noble.)

ALFRED. I'm ready! Hello, Arthur!
CARTE. *(Ushering him back offstage.)* Your Royal Highness ...
ALFRED. Oh. *(To GILBERT –)* Sorry! *(He exits.)*
GILBERT. *(Fuming.)* Rutland!

(RUTLAND enters wearing a suit of "fat man" padding, which he normally wears under his costume for the role of Pooh-Bah.)

RUTLAND. All set.
GILBERT. Good God. What's that?!
RUTLAND. The padding.
GILBERT. I know it's the padding, you fat-head. Where's the costume?
RUTLAND. They're fixing it. I split a seam.
GILBERT. God Almighty.

(At this moment, VIOLET hurries in from the wings, still buttoning her costume, and takes her place between JESSIE and SYBIL. Her lateness is very obvious.)

GILBERT. How kind of you to join us. Miss Russell. I hope it wasn't an inconvenience. *(No answer.)* Are you ready?!
VIOLET. Yes sir.
GILBERT. Sullivan!?
SULLIVAN. *(From the pit.)* Ready!
GILBERT. Lights!

[MUSIC CUE #12A/B: SO PLEASE YOU, SIR]

(*SULLIVAN raises his baton, and the "Mikado" medley*
   begins. Throughout the medley, SULLIVAN is visible
   from the waist up, as he conducts the orchestra.
The medley begins with "So Please You, Sir, a stacatto
   tour de force of tremendous difficulty. The roles for
   the medley are as follows: RUTLAND / Poo-Bah;
   GEORGE / Pish-Tush; DURWARD / Nanki-Poo;
   VIOLET / Yum-Yum; JESSIE / Pitti-Sing; and
   SYBIL / Peep-Bo.)

    VIOLET, SYBIL and JESSIE. (Yum-Yum, Peep-Bo,
Pitti-Sing.)
SO PLEASE YOU, SIR, WE MUCH REGRET
IF WE HAVE FAILED IN ETIQUETTE
TOWARDS A MAN OF RANK SO HIGH
WE SHALL KNOW BETTER BY AND BY.
    GILBERT. (*Breaking in.*) No No *NO!* Mush! It's just
mush!

(*The music halts, followed by a deadly silence.*)

    GILBERT. My god, you sound like amateurs. I can't
hear a word! (*Pause.*) Miss *Russell* ...
    VIOLET. Yes sir.
    GILBERT. I would have thought, Miss Russell, that in
light of your debut with this company, you might have
made the Herculean effort of practising. Apparently, that
is not the case. "So *please* you sir we *much* re-*gret*." "So
please you sir —" Tongue tongue *tongue.* My *God!* (*JESSIE*
sighs audibly.) Then again, we do have a whole eight
hours, so let's waste all of our time and practice it
together. Quarter-time! One, two, one, two. (*He claps the*
quarter-time rhythm and sings it along with them —)
    GILBERT, JESSIE, SYBIL & VIOLET.
SO PLEASE YOU SIR, WE MUCH REGRET
IF WE HAVE FAILED IN ET-I-QUETTE, —
    GILBERT. Half-time! On the tongue! (*Still*
clapping—)

GILBERT, JESSIE, SYBIL & VIOLET.
SO PLEASE YOU SIR, WE MUCH REGRET
IF WE HAVE FAILED IN ET-I-QUETTE, –
    GILBERT. Tempo! (*Still clapping, at full speed* –)
    GILBERT, JESSIE, SYBIL & VIOLET.
SO PLEASE YOU SIR, WE MUCH REGRET
IF WE HAVE FAILED IN ET-I-QUETTE, –
TO-WARDS A MAN OF RANK SO HIGH
WE SHALL KNOW BETTER BY AND BY.
    GILBERT. All right, all right. Now that's the way you
should have practiced it. If, Miss Russell, you'd cared at
all.
    SULLIVAN. (*Highly annoyed.*) I'm sure it'll be fine,
girls.
    GILBERT. From the *top*.

(*The GIRLS return to their positions surrounding Pooh-
Bah and the song begins again, this time continuing
to the end.*)

    VIOLET, SYBIL and JESSIE. (Yum-Yum, Peep-Bo,
Pitti-Sing.)
SO PLEASE YOU, SIR, WE MUCH REGRET
IF WE HAVE FAILED IN ETIQUETTE
TOWARDS A MAN OF RANK SO HIGH
WE SHALL KNOW BETTER BY AND BY.
    VIOLET. (Yum-Yum.)
BUT YOUTH, OF COURSE, MUST HAVE ITS FLING,
SO PARDON US, SO PARDON US,
    JESSIE. (Pitti-Sing.)
AND DON'T, IN GIRLHOOD'S HAPPY SPRING,
BE HARD ON US, BE HARD ON US,
IF WE'RE INCLINED TO DANCE AND SING.
TRA LA LA, ETC. (*Dancing.*)
    CHORUS OF GIRLS.
BUT YOUTH, OF COURSE, MUST HAVE ITS FLING,
    ETC.

RUTLAND. (Pooh-Bah.)
I THINK YOU OUGHT TO RECOLLECT
YOU CANNOT SHOW TOO MUCH RESPECT
TOWARDS THE HIGHLY TITLED FEW;
BUT NOBODY DOES, AND WHY SHOULD YOU?
THAT YOUTH AT US SHOULD HAVE ITS FLING,
IS HARD ON US, IS HARD ON US;
TO OUR PREROGATIVE WE CLING –
SO PARDON US. SO PARDON US,
IF WE DECLINE TO DANCE AND SING.
TRA LA LA, ETC. (*Dancing.*)
    CHORUS OF GIRLS.
BUT YOUTH, OF COURSE, MUST HAVE ITS FLING,
ETC.

[MUSIC CUE #13: YOUNG MAN, DESPAIR]

(*The medley continues with the strong, accented
introduction to "Young Man Despair," featuring
RUTLAND, GEORGE and DURWARD. After
RUTLAND begins singing, GEORGE realizes that
ALFRED is missing, and signals to him to enter –
"Psst!" ALFRED hurries on, carrying a large,
tasseled sunshade on a pole. As Pooh-Bah's servant,
he is supposed to keep the sunshade positioned over
Pooh-Bah's head – a task that he fails utterly to do. He
begins by holding it over GEORGE. GEORGE
motions to him, and he runs to RUTLAND, who is
seated, and holds it over RUTLAND's head. When
RUTLAND rises to his feet, he is enveloped by the
sunshade, which ALFRED neglects to raise. And so it
continues. When RUTLAND marches in one
direction, ALFRED marches in the other, bumping
into him. When ALFRED moves RUTLAND's chair,
he drops it with a bang. During the second verse,
ALFRED begins to enjoy himself and bounces in
rhythm on the balls of his feet. The tassels bounce
along with him – until RUTLAND and GILBERT*

simultaneously grab him by the shoulders. On the final chorus, ALFRED at last marches in the right direction — until the others turn and ALFRED marches offstage. GILBERT bellows "That way" and ALFRED rushes back on. The last straw occurs during the final notes of music: ALFRED, exhausted, lowers the sunshade, and RUTLAND, bowing to GEORGE, backs into the pointed end of it and screams.)

SONG (Quartet)

RUTLAND. (Pooh-Bah.)
YOUNG MAN, DESPAIR,
LIKEWISE GO TO,
YUM-YUM THE FAIR
YOU MUST NOT WOO.
IT WILL NOT DO:
I'M SORRY FOR YOU.
YOU VERY IMPERFECT ABLUTIONER!
THIS VERY DAY
FROM SCHOOL YUM-YUM
WILL WEND HER WAY,
AND HOMEWARD COME,
WITH BEAT OF DRUM
AND A RUM-TUM-TUM,
TO WED THE LORD HIGH EXECUTIONER!
AND THE BRASS WILL CRASH,
AND THE TRUMPETS BRAY,
AND THEY'LL CUT A DASH
ON THEIR WEDDING DAY.
SHE'LL TODDLE AWAY, AS ALL AVER,
WITH THE LORD HIGH EXECUTIONER!
    ALL.
AND THE BRASS WILL CRASH, ETC.
    RUTLAND. (Pooh-Bah.)
IT'S A HOPELESS CASE,
AS YOU MAY SEE,

AND IN YOUR PLACE
AWAY I'D FLEE; BUT DON'T BLAME ME –
I'M SORRY TO BE
OF YOUR PLEASURE A DIMINUTIONER.
THEY'LL VOW THEIR PACT
EXTREMELY SOON,
IN POINT OF FACT
THIS AFTERNOON.
HER HONEYMOON
WITH THAT BUFFOON
AT SEVEN COMMENCES, SO *YOU* SHUN HER!
    ALL.
AND THE BRASS WILL CRASH, ETC.
    GILBERT. (*In the pause.*) God almighty!

(*As GILBERT fumes, the three GIRLS take center stage
again, for the start of their famous trio, "Three Little
Maids from School."*)

[MUSIC CUE #14A/B: THREE LITTLE MAIDS
FROM SCHOOL]

SONG (Trio)
THE THREE.
THREE LITTLE MAIDS FROM SCHOOL ARE WE,
PERT AS A SCHOOL-GIRL WELL CAN BE,
FILLED TO THE BRIM WITH GIRLISH GLEE,
[*Suddenly demure, fluttering fans.*]
THREE LITTLE MAIDS FROM SCHOOL!
    GILBERT. (*Overlapping.*) Fans up. Up! Fans!
Dammit. Flutter your fan! HOLD IT!

(*The music grinds to a halt. Pause*)

    GILBERT. Miss Russell ...
    VIOLET. Yes sir.
    GILBERT. Have you read the stage direction to this
piece, Miss Russell?

VIOLET. I – I think so. (*She glances into the pit, looking for support from SULLIVAN.*)

GILBERT. You *think* so. Well that's wonderful. You think so. And what does it say?

SULLIVAN. Demurely!

GILBERT. Sullivan.

VIOLET. ... Demurely.

GILBERT. It says "Suddenly demure, fluttering fans." Do you think you can flutter?

VIOLET. (*Hurt.*) I think – Yes.

GILBERT. Well go ahead. (*She does.*) No no *no!* Here, give it to me! (*He grabs her fan.*) Like this. (*He poses and flutters demurely.*)

VIOLET. I see.

GILBERT. Try it. (*She does.*) My God ...

SULLIVAN. (*Indignantly, calling out.*) It looks all right to me!

(*A tense pause.*)

GILBERT. I'm so glad.

SULLIVAN. (*Ascending to the stage.*) Gilbert, for heaven's sake!

GILBERT. Are you speaking to me?

SULLIVAN. Let's just get on with it, shall we.

GILBERT. Just – get on with it ...?

SULLIVAN. Yes.

GILBERT. (*Quietly.*) I see. Just, get on with it. Good idea. After all, I have only been here six weeks, working night and day. But let's not direct this part. Let's just get on with it. Fine. Please do so. I will be in the dressing room if you need me. (*He hobbles into the wings and disappears.*)

(*Stunned silence. SULLIVAN looks at CARTE. CARTE rolls his eyes and walks off to find GILBERT. No one else moves.*)

SULLIVAN. (*At last; slowly.*) Well. Ahem. Shall we, uh, pick it up?

(*Silence. No one moves. A long, mournful pause.*)

SULLIVAN. Come on now, ladies. Miss Russell. (*No response.*) Violet.
VIOLET. (*Pause. She looks up at him.*) All right.
SULLIVAN. From the beginning please. Cellier?

(*The three little maids take their positions and the song begins — a very sad affair altogether. VIOLET is deeply hurt, SYBIL is demoralized and JESSIE is angry, snapping her fan open and closed with a vengeance. Their emotions, of course, are totally at odds with the intent of the song. SULLIVAN remains onstage as CELLIER conducts the orchestra.*)

<u>SONG</u> (Trio)
THE THREE.
THREE LITTLE MAIDS FROM SCHOOL ARE WE,
PERT AS A SCHOOL-GIRL WELL CAN BE,
FILLED TO THE BRIM WITH GIRLISH GLEE,
[*Suddenly demure, fluttering fans.*]
THREE LITTLE MAIDS FROM SCHOOL!
  VIOLET. (Yum-Yum.)
EVERYTHING IS A SOURCE OF FUN.
(*Chuckle.*)
  SYBIL. (Peep-Bo.)
NOBODY'S SAFE, FOR WE CARE FOR NONE!
(*Chuckle.*)
  JESSIE. (Pitti-Sing.)
LIFE IS A JOKE THAT'S JUST BEGUN!
(*Chuckle.*)
  THE THREE.
THREE LITTLE MAIDS FROM SCHOOL!
  SULLIVAN. Come on, girls!

ALL. (*Dancing.*)
THREE LITTLE MAIDS WHO, ALL UNWARY
COME FROM A LADIES' SEMINARY
FREED FROM ITS GENIUS TUTELARY
    THE THREE. (*Suddenly demure, fluttering fans.*)
THREE LITTLE MAIDS FROM SCHOOL!
    VIOLET. (Yum-Yum.)
ONE LITTLE MAID IS A BRIDE, YUM-YUM –
    SYBIL. (Peep-Bo.)
TWO LITTLE MAIDS IN ATTENDANCE COME –
    JESSIE. (Pitti-Sing.)
THREE LITTLE MAIDS IS THE TOTAL SUM.
    THE THREE.
THREE LITTLE MAIDS FROM SCHOOL!
    VIOLET. (Yum-Yum.)
FROM THREE LITTLE MAIDS TAKE ONE AWAY.
    SYBIL. (Peep-Bo.)
TWO LITTLE MAIDS REMAIN, AND THEY –
    JESSIE. (Pitti-Sing.)
WON'T HAVE TO WAIT VERY LONG, THEY SAY–
    THE THREE.
THREE LITTLE MAIDS FROM SCHOOL!

(*Suddenly, GILBERT marches in from the wings.*)

GILBERT. *Joyful,* dammit!

(*The GIRLS light up immediately. CARTE, back again, shoots SULLIVAN a wry glance. And as GILBERT scrutinizes the girls intently, the song continues to the end with confidence and high spirits.*)

ALL. (*Dancing.*)
THREE LITTLE MAIDS WHO, ALL UNWARY,
COME FROM A LADIES' SEMINARY,
FREED FROM ITS GENIUS TUTELARY
    THE THREE. (*Suddenly demure, fluttering, fans.*)
THREE LITTLE MAIDS FROM SCHOOL!

[MUSIC CUE #15: TRANSITION TO SCENE 7]

Scene 7

Gilbert and Sullivan's dressing room. A few minutes later.
GILBERT and SULLIVAN enter together. SULLIVAN closes the door and looks at GILBERT.
Pause.

SULLIVAN. Now, of course, you feel contrite.

GILBERT. Hardly.

SULLIVAN. You were pretty hard on them, you know. Especially that ... new girl. In fact, it seemed to me you were actually picking on her –

GILBERT. Sullivan ... what do you think of her? Miss Russell.

SULLIVAN. I think she's wonderful. Voice. Looks. She has everything. Don't you?

GILBERT. I don't know.

SULLIVAN. She's an excellent choice, I assure you.

GILBERT. Mm.

SULLIVAN. And I must admit, I thought you handled Alfred pretty well. Very big of you.

GILBERT. Very small of him.

SULLIVAN. Now I'm sure he appreciates it. Believe me.

GILBERT. Well I don't like it. Not a bit of it.

SULLIVAN. Oh come on now, where's your sense of fun?

GILBERT. That's it. That's it! To you this is just a lot of fun. That's it exactly. I have slaved like a dumb beast for nineteen years and you call it fun. It's a good thing no one dies onstage tonight or you'd laugh your head off. I'm sure you would be doubled over if Yum-Yum contracted syphilis and went mad.

SULLIVAN. For heaven's sake — !

GILBERT. If this were opening night of *Ivanhoe* and I asked you if one of my friends could just toss off one of your little ditties ...

SULLIVAN. That's a different thing entirely.

GILBERT. Aha. Why? I'll tell you why. Because you have no respect for anything we have ever done.

SULLIVAN. How can you say that?

GILBERT. To this day you haven't the slightest appreciation of the balance, the reassuring proportion that I have slaved for in every plot that I have ever written. That, Sullivan, is your art. A beginning, a middle, and an end. And damn difficult it is too.

SULLIVAN. (*Pause.*) It's all a matter of ... flexibility, isn't it?

GILBERT. Don't start on one of your "words."

SULLIVAN. But that's the key, isn't it? Flex-i-bility.

GILBERT. God in heaven.

SULLIVAN. The plays that we write together are flexible. A grand opera is not flexible. I am flexible. You are not flexible.

GILBERT. I can't take it.

SULLIVAN. Which is why you have never been knighted. Though you will be if you're nice to Alfred.

GILBERT. I will not waste my life toadying to Lord Jackass.

SULLIVAN. Because you are not flexible.

GILBERT. Flexible? You must be made of India rubber.

SULLIVAN. I am flexible.

GILBERT. Do not say that word one more time in my presence!

SULLIVAN. Let me say this —

GILBERT. And don't get pompous.

SULLIVAN. I was only going to say that you have increased your chances for a knighthood ten-fold by being ... reasonable for a change.

GILBERT. Bloody hell.

SULLIVAN. (*With relish.*) Sir William Schwenck Gilbert.

GILBERT. There is nothing funny about "Schwenck." It happens to be swathed in nobility.

SULLIVAN. Of course there's nothing funny about it. I love it. Schwenck.

GILBERT. Stop it.

SULLIVAN. (*Savoring it.*) Sir Schwenck.

GILBERT. It's cosmopolitan. You wouldn't know that, born in Lambeth –

SULLIVAN. (*Reveling, dancing about.*) *Lord* Schwenck. *Duke* Schwenck. *Prince* Schwenck! *Schwenck! Schwenck! Schwenck!* Ha-ha! *SCHWENCK!*

GILBERT. (*Overlapping.*) Stop it, you're going MAD! You're losing CONTROL OF YOURSELF! Bloody *hell* ...

(*Suddenly mid-shout, SULLIVAN is seized with a sharp pain in his liver. It stops him dead in his tracks – a gasp, his hand to his abdomen, then a cry of pain.*)

GILBERT. ... Arthur! (*He runs to him.*) Arthur! Sit down, sit down man. Here ... (*Gently he helps SULLIVAN to a chair.*) Are you all right? ... Here ... (*He grabs the ottoman that he uses for his bad leg and puts it in front of Sullivan's chair.*) ... feet up ... Arthur?

SULLIVAN. (*In pain.*) Mm.

GILBERT. Shall I call a doctor? Who's your doctor?!

SULLIVAN. (*Barely audible.*) No.

GILBERT. (*Running to the liquor table.*) Here. Wait. (*He pours some water into a glass and hurries back.*) Some water. Drink this. Sullivan? ... Let me call your doctor. Hm? Arthur?

SULLIVAN. No ... There's nothing ... he can do. (*He takes a sip of the water.*)

(Pause. All is quiet now.)

SULLIVAN. I, uh ...
GILBERT. Don't talk.

(Pause. GILBERT, frightened to death, watches SULLIVAN intently for several seconds.)

GILBERT. Better?
SULLIVAN. *(Shaking his head yes.)* Mm.

(After several more seconds – it seems a very long time – SULLIVAN sighs and begins to breathe more easily. Seeing this, GILBERT sighs deeply.)

GILBERT. *(Still shaken.)* That's quite a fright you gave me.
SULLIVAN. *(Quietly.)* Sorry.
GILBERT. What do you do for these things?
SULLIVAN. Just wait. Sit quietly.
GILBERT. Well be quiet then. Close your eyes.
SULLIVAN. ... I shouldn't get worked up ... I don't mind it too much, unless I'm alone.
GILBERT. Well you shouldn't be alone.
SULLIVAN. In Monte Carlo ... I was alone then ... I thought I was going to die.
GILBERT. Rubbish.
SULLIVAN. I did.
GILBERT. Well you're not going to die. I'm sure you could not be so unfair to me as to do that. *(Pause.)* Now go to sleep.
SULLIVAN. Don't be silly –
GILBERT. Go to sleep! I order you.
SULLIVAN. *(Getting up.)* But there's so much to –
GILBERT. Will you sit down! My God, you're like a child.
SULLIVAN. William –

GILBERT. Down!

(*SULLIVAN sits down.*)

GILBERT. Now take off your shoes and put your feet up.
SULLIVAN. Don't be ridiculous.
GILBERT. Sullivan –
SULLIVAN. My feet are none of your business.
GILBERT. Take off your shoes!

(*SULLIVAN growls and reluctantly begins taking them off.*)

GILBERT. It's no wonder you have attacks. I'm surprised you're not comatose ...

(*SULLIVAN puts his feet on the ottoman. Without a word, GILBERT positions himself beside Sullivan's feet, which he then picks up, cradling one ankle in each hand, facing front.*)

SULLIVAN. (*Startled.*) What are you doing?
GILBERT. Holding your feet.
SULLIVAN. (*Struggling.*) Are you mad? ...
GILBERT. Lie still!
SULLIVAN. Gilbert! ...

(*SULLIVAN struggles for another moment, then gives up.*)

SULLIVAN. All right. Why are you holding my feet?
GILBERT. Because it's very relaxing.
SULLIVAN. You find it relaxing to hold my feet?
GILBERT. Not me. You, you idiot.
SULLIVAN. (*Pause.*) I don't like it.
GILBERT. It takes a while. (*Pause.*) When I am very low, Kitty holds my feet. It works wonders.

SULLIVAN. That's because you have gout.

GILBERT. Because it's relaxing. Now close your eyes.

(*Pause. SULLIVAN closes his eyes and sighs deeply.*)

SULLIVAN. What if someone walks in?

GILBERT. I'll drop them.

(*Long pause. SULLIVAN finally relaxes. He begins to get drowsy.*)

GILBERT. Well?

SULLIVAN. (*Half-smiling.*) Divine.

GILBERT. (*Chuckling.*) It is, isn't it.

SULLIVAN. (*Chuckling.*) Yes ... It's ridiculous ... But it's heavenly ... (*He yawns.*) She'll think I've gone mad.

GILBERT. Who?

SULLIVAN. Violet. (*His eyes flash open, realizing what he's said.*)

GILBERT. Who's Violet?

SULLIVAN. Now I've done it. Now you know.

GILBERT. Know what?

SULLIVAN. The girl. My ... friend.

GILBERT. I only know one girl named Violet and she's in the show.

SULLIVAN. Well?

GEORGE. (*A double-take.*) Not ... Violet?!

SULLIVAN. (*Gleefully.*) Yes.

GILBERT. Violet *Russell?*

SULLIVAN. That's her.

GILBERT. (*Dropping Sullivan's feet.*) I don't believe it.

SULLIVAN. (*Happily.*) Neither do I.

GILBERT. I don't believe it ...

SULLIVAN. You're not going to be jealous?

GILBERT. Sullivan, have you lost your senses?

SULLIVAN. All right, all right, she's young – I know that. But she has a head, Gilbert.

GILBERT. It's impossible.

SULLIVAN. It's true.

GILBERT. You're baiting me. It's a joke.

SULLIVAN. (*With an edge.*) Gilbert. It's not a joke. You're the first to know.

GILBERT. Do you have any notion of what you're doing?

SULLIVAN. Of course I do. She's a darling.

GILBERT. Sullivan ... (*He doesn't know how to begin.*)

SULLIVAN. You know, I think you're actually jealous –

GILBERT. Sullivan, what do you know about her? Have you met her family?

SULLIVAN. They're in Australia. I suppose I'll meet them –

GILBERT. I mean her background. Her ... circle ...

SULLIVAN. You're getting a little snobbish, aren't you?

GILBERT. (*Vehemently.*) Do you know anything about her background?!

SULLIVAN. (*Startled.*) She was a singer, in Australia. Arrived here a few months ago ...

GILBERT. Sullivan – (*Pause. Quietly; painfully.*) She was a dancing-girl. In a music hall.

SULLIVAN. (*Incredulous.*) What? Who told you that?

GILBERT. It's true.

SULLIVAN. She – she sang ballads in a music hall, she told me that ...

GILBERT. In her knickers.

SULLIVAN. That's a *lie!*

GILBERT. I saw her myself.

SULLIVAN. You did not. You're mistaken!

GILBERT. I saw her I tell you!

SULLIVAN. That's impossible!

GILBERT. Sullivan, now calm down.

SULLIVAN. Get away from me –
GILBERT. Don't get excited!
SULLIVAN. I am not excited!
GILBERT. Don't you see, I can't sit back and let you hang yourself –
SULLIVAN. You're out of your *mind!!*

(*Pause. They stare at each other.*)

SULLIVAN. What's the matter with you?
GILBERT. Sullivan. I saw her.
SULLIVAN. You couldn't have.
GILBERT. It's the truth.
SULLIVAN. Just stop it!
GILBERT. The girl shook her bottom in front of a –
SULLIVAN. That's a lie!
GILBERT. Will you listen to me!! (*Pause.*) She'll make you miserable.
SULLIVAN. She will not!
GILBERT. Just imagine – taking her to Sandringham, with all your dukes and princes –
SULLIVAN. I don't care!
GILBERT. Well you will! Believe me, Sullivan. Believe me ...
SULLIVAN. Don't speak to me. Don't ever speak to me again. (*Furiously, he pulls on his shoes.*) You are jealous of me! You are jealous of everything I have ever done!
GILBERT. Confront her! Ask her a few questions!
SULLIVAN. I should have listened to my friends. They told me you were no good. And I defended you!
GILBERT. Sullivan take hold of yourself! Just *calm down!* You'll have an *attack!*

(*By this time, SULLIVAN has grabbed his coat and is heading for the door.*)

GILBERT. Where are you going? ... Where do you think you're going?!

SULLIVAN. Out! For good. So you may conduct the orchestra. You may call off the performance. I won't be here, and I don't care!

GILBERT. You can't do that.

SULLIVAN. I shall do as I please!

GILBERT. Don't be an idiot!

SULLIVAN. (*Pause. At the door.*) If I could destroy every note of music that I ever wrote for your ridiculous rhymes, I would do it this instant.

GILBERT. (*Stung.*) Sullivan.

(*SULLIVAN stalks out the door right – the one leading to the alley – slamming it behind him.*
GILBERT is dumbstruck, unable to move for a moment. Then he hurries to the door.)

GILBERT. Sullivan! Sullivan get back in here! *SULLIVAN! (Nothing. GILBERT closes the door and hobbles back into the room, grief-stricken. He looks around the empty room.)* Sullivan ...

(*The lights fade.*)

END OF ACT I

ACT II

Scene 1

The Savoy stage. The same day, late afternoon.

[MUSIC CUE #17: WOULD YOU KNOW THE KIND
OF MAID]

*When the lights come up, the orchestra begins the short
introduction to "Would You Know the Kind of Maid"
from Princess Ida. The stage is empty except for two
or three cane chairs. COURTICE, playing Cyril,
springs gaily onto the stage in medieval costume (the
sillier the better). In his usual fashion, COURTICE
sings his heart out. Considering the song, the result is
slightly absurd, which is just what GILBERT
intended when he wrote it.*

SONG (Solo.)
COURTICE. (Cyril.)
WOULD YOU KNOW THE KIND OF MAID
SETS MY HEART AFLAME-A?
EYES MUST BE DOWNCAST AND STAID,
CHEEKS MUST FLUSH FOR SHAME-A!
SHE MAY NEITHER DANCE NOR SING,
BUT, DEMURE IN EVERYTHING,
HANG HER HEAD IN MODEST WAY,
WITH POUTING LIPS THAT SEEM TO SAY,
"OH, KISS ME, KISS ME, KISS ME, KISS ME,
THOUGH I DIE OF SHAME-A!"
PLEASE, YOU, THAT'S THE KIND OF MAID
SETS MY HEART AFLAME-A!

(*About this time, GILBERT wanders onto the stage. Thoroughly miserable, he sits down listlessly, chin in hand, and muses, oblivious to Courtice's performance. COURTICE continues singing, but can't help glancing at GILBERT, wondering what he's doing wrong. And the more worried he becomes, the more he hams it up.*)

COURTICE. (Cyril.)
WHEN A MAID IS BOLD AND GAY
WITH A TONGUE GOES CLANG-A,
FLAUNTING IT IN BRAVE ARRAY,
MAIDEN MAY GO HANG-A
SUNFLOWER GAY AND HOLLYHOCK
NEVER SHALL MY GARDEN STOCK;
MINE THE BLUSHING ROSE OF MAY,
WITH POUTING LIPS THAT SEEM TO SAY,
"OH, KISS ME, KISS ME, KISS ME, KISS ME,
THOUGH I DIE FOR SHAME-A!"
PLEASE YOU, THAT'S THE KIND OF MAID
SETS MY HEART AFLAME-A!

(*When the song is over, COURTICE waits for GILBERT's explosion. GILBERT, however, is lost in thought.*)

COURTICE. (*With trepidation.*) Mr. Gilbert? ...
GEORGE. Hm? Oh. Very nice. Keep it up.

(*Before COURTICE can reply, we hear CARTE bellowing offstage, left, "William!? ... William!!?"*)

GILBERT. (*To COURTICE.*) Excuse me. (*Immediately he gets up and starts hobbling to the wings, right, obviously avoiding CARTE. He almost makes it, when CARTE stalks in from the left.*)
CARTE. William!
GILBERT. (*Turning.*) Ah, there you are.
CARTE. Courtice. (*He motions him off the stage.*)

COURTICE. Right. (*Exits.*)

CARTE. (*Bearing down on GILBERT.*) All right, William, enough is enough. Where is he?

GILBERT. Where is who?

CARTE. Where is Arthur, dammit! Tell me this instant!

GILBERT. I wouldn't know.

CARTE. You had an argument, didn't you? Admit it, William. Admit it!

GILBERT. How would you like to be even shorter than you are now?

CARTE. William ...

GILBERT. We ... disagreed.

CARTE. I knew it! Dammit all, I knew it! You told him about the girl, didn't you? And then you got stubborn. Oh, I can see it all.

GILBERT. I don't believe it's any of your business.

CARTE. My business ...? William, the show starts in two hours! And the Queen. My God, William, the Queen! She's expecting him. What if he doesn't show up?

GILBERT. He won't.

CARTE. He won't?

GILBERT. He was very explicit. He said he was through.

CARTE. Oh my God.

GILBERT. (*Sadly.*) This time I think he meant it.

CARTE. Oh my God! How could you do this?!

GILBERT. Me? Sullivan's the one who walked out!

CARTE. WELL OF COURSE HE WALKED OUT! ... Don't you understand anything? We are a fabric, William. A bloody balancing act. Pull one of us out and we're on the floor. Why do you think I've put up with all your fuss and tantrums? Hm? Because I like it?

GILBERT. ... You don't?

CARTE. From the moment I brought you two together I knew it was trouble. But I said to myself, "Now wait a minute, Carte. Just hold your horses. This could be

special. This could be worth the candle." And dammit
all, I was right!

GILBERT. Carte –

CARTE. Don't "Carte" me, William, with your sheep-
dog eyes. I know you. If this is the end, then so be it. Fine.
But just remember, you have brought it on yourself. By
alienating the best composer – and the best producer – in
the whole bloody country! (*Walks off.*)

(*GILBERT, depressed, sits down, musing again. After a
few seconds, ALFRED enters tentatively from the
wings. GILBERT doesn't see him. ALFRED comes
forward, a few more steps.*)

ALFRED. Knock knock. (*GILBERT looks up.*) Sorry
to bother you ...

GILBERT. (*Not unkindly.*) Yes?

ALFRED. I thought ... perhaps, if you had a minute ...
My lines ...? Arthur, you see, thought if we practiced a
little ...

(*Pause. GILBERT looks at him and thinks of
SULLIVAN.*)

GILBERT. Arthur. Yes, of course. (*He stands up.*)
Let's do it. (*During the following, GILBERT places two
chairs close together in the center of the stage.*)

ALFRED. Really?

GILBERT. Why not.

ALFRED. Now?

GILBERT. Would you prefer tomorrow?

ALFRED. Oh no no no. Right. I'm all set!

GILBERT. Fine. (*He takes a deep breath – he has a
job to do.*) Now first of all –

ALFRED. (*Slightly giddy; his old self again.*) Oh,
this should be fun.

GILBERT. Have a seat.

ALFRED. Right.

(They both sit.)

GILBERT. Now this is a trio —

ALFRED. I know.

GILBERT. It occurs in the second act of *H.M.S. Pinafore* —

ALFRED. Do you know that's one of my favorites. Always had been.

GILBERT. Thank you.

ALFRED. *(Singing.)* "I am the monarch of the sea —" I could do that one.

GILBERT. Maybe next time. Now Sullivan ... Arthur... tells me you know your lines and your cues.

ALFRED. *(Confidently.)* I think so.

GILBERT. And the dancing?

ALFRED. Oh yes.

GILBERT. Excellent. Now the setting. You are Sir Joseph Porter, Admiral of the Fleet.

ALFRED. *(Confidentially.)* You know, I am. Admiral of the Fleet. I mean, really.

GILBERT. Yes, I know.

ALFRED. Quite a coincidence, I think.

GILBERT. Amazing.

ALFRED. Do you know I went round the world once in my own ship, the *Galatea*. Went to India —

GILBERT. Alfred.

ALFRED. Oh. Sorry.

GILBERT. Now — in the play, Sir Joseph is in love with a girl below his social rank named Josephine. She in turn secretly loves a man below *hers,* a simple sailor, named Ralph. Now in the the song Sir Joseph assures the girl that love can level social ranks —

ALFRED. Hear hear! I like that.

GILBERT. Thank you. Now, I shall recite the lines preceding your first entrance, and I want you to *recite* your first line, on cue. Don't sing it.

ALFRED. Got it.

GILBERT. All right. Ahem. "Never mind the why and wherefore, Love can level ranks and therefore, Though his —"

ALFRED. (*Overlapping, with gusto.*) "*Ring* the merry bells on board-ship, *Rend* the air with warbling wild —"

GILBERT. Not yet! (*Pause.*) That's not your cue.

ALFRED. Oh.

GILBERT. Do you know your cue?

ALFRED. (*Thinking.*) Something, something ... "plain."

GILBERT. "Your fortune poor and plain."

ALFRED. That's it. I, uh, ... I was excited.

GILBERT. If you sing before your cue, you'll ruin everything.

ALFRED. "Plain." I remember now.

GILBERT. "Plain." All right.

(*ALFRED concentrates.*)

GILBERT. "Never mind the why and wherefore, Love can level ranks and therefore, Though his lordship's station's mighty, Though stupendous be his brain — "

ALFRED. "*Ring* the merry bells on board-ship, *Rend* the air with warbling wild —"

GILBERT. (*Overlapping.*) No no NO!

ALFRED. You said "plain."

GILBERT. I said "brain!"

ALFRED. Oh. I thought you said "plain."

GILBERT. "Brain."

ALFRED. (*Sweating.*) It sounds like "plain."

GILBERT. Your cue is "fortune *poor* and *plain.*"

ALFRED. I managed it all right with Arthur.

GILBERT. I'm sure.

ALFRED. Can I jump to the solo? Please? You know, the bit by myself ...

GILBERT. All right.

ALFRED. I'll sing it. I – I do better with the rhythm. Gets me going.

GILBERT. Fine, sing it. But wait for the cue. Ahem. "With a man who owns her love." ... (*No response.*) That was your cue.

ALFRED. I thought it was "plain."

GILBERT. For the *solo.*

ALFRED. Oh right right right! That's it! I was confused. All right. "Owns her love," beat beat – (*Singing –*)
"NEVER MIND THE WHERE AND WHYFORE
LOVE CAN LEVEL RANKS AND THYFORE –" ...
Thyfore?

GILBERT. Alfred!

ALFRED. (*Sweating bullets.*) You've made me extremely nervous!

GILBERT. Don't get excited! An actor has to think while he is acting.

ALFRED. Right. (*Suddenly he remembers Violet's advice.*) Right! That's it! I am Sir Joseph. I'm all set. I am sir Joseph, I am Sir Joseph, I am Sir Joseph ...

GILBERT. Now recite your lines and think of them as you say them.

ALFRED. Ahem ... "Never mind the where and whyfore" ...

GILBERT. "Why and wherefore."

ALFRED. Hm?

GILBERT. "*Why* and *where*fore." You have it backwards.

ALFRED. "Why and ..." Oh – yes yes yes, that's it! "Why and *where*fore." I had it backwards. I'm all set now. Ready to go. (*Desperately –*) I'll sing it. Ahem. "Owns her love," beat beat – (*Singing –*)
"NEVER MIND THE WHY AND WHEREFORE,
LOVE CAN LEVEL RANKS AND THEREFORE,
THOUGH YOUR NAUTICAL RELATIONS
IN MY SOMETHING SOMETHING SOMETHING I
    KNEW IT THIS *MORNING!!!*

GILBERT. Alfred –
ALFRED. I did! I swear it!
GILBERT. Alfred – !

(At this moment, RUTLAND and SYBIL enter from the wings, chatting.)

ALFRED. Rutland! Sybil! *(To GILBERT.)* If I could sing it, with the music – !
GILBERT. If you don't know you lines –
ALFRED. I can do it! Believe me –
RUTLAND. May we be of assistance, Your Royal Highness?
GILBERT. Forget it. *(He begins to walk off.)*
ALFRED. Wait! please! *(To RUTLAND and SYBIL.)* My song, you see – with you two – well I want to practice it–
GILBERT. Alfred – !
SYBIL. Well why not?
RUTLAND. Sounds fair to me –
GILBERT. We have been practicing it.
ALFRED. With the music. It's so much easier –
SYBIL. Well of course it is.
GILBERT. It is not.
RUTLAND. It is for some of us.
SYBIL. It really is.
GILBERT. *(Pause.)* All right, all right.
ALFRED. Ohhh – *(Relief.)*
GILBERT. Cellier!
CELLIER. *(From the pit.)* Right here.
GILBERT. Trio from *Pinafore*. At tempo.
ALFRED. *(To RUTLAND and SYBIL.)* This is awfully kind of you –
RUTLAND. *(Graciously.)* Not at all. Now just relax.
SYBIL. You'll be just fine –
GILBERT. Will you sing the song?!
ALFRED. Right. *(He moves into position.)* Lights!

(The performance lights come up. GILBERT is not amused.)
    [MUSIC CUE #18: TRIO: NEVER MIND THE WHY
        AND WHEREFORE]

(CELLIER begins the introduction to "Never Mind the Why and Wherefore" and the three singers – RUTLAND as Captain Corcoran, SYBIL as Josephine and ALFRED as Sir Joseph – come forward in rhythm.
ALFRED is a bit tentative at first, but RUTLAND and SYBIL help him along, with nods for cues and restraining shakes of the head when necessary. By the middle of the song ALFRED is doing fine, and by the end he performs his solo and the dancing with gusto, letter-perfect. RUTLAND and SYBIL are obviously delighted for him.)

SONG (Trio)
RUTLAND. (Captain.)
NEVER MIND THE WHY AND WHEREFORE,
LOVE CAN LEVEL RANKS, AND THEREFORE,
THOUGH HIS LORDSHIP'S STATION'S MIGHTY,
THOUGH STUPENDOUS BE HIS BRAIN,
THOUGH YOUR TASTES ARE MEAN AND FLIGHTY
AND YOUR FORTUNE POOR AND PLAIN.
    RUTLAND. (Captain.) & **ALFRED.** (Sir Jos.)
RING THE MERRY BELLS ON BOARD-SHIP
REND THE AIR WITH WARBLING WILD,
FOR THE UNION OF HIS/MY LORDSHIP
WITH A HUMBLE CAPTAIN'S CHILD!
    RUTLAND. (Captain.)
FOR A HUMBLE CAPTAIN'S DAUGHTER –
    SYBIL. (Josephine.)
FOR A GALLANT CAPTAIN'S DAUGHTER
    ALFRED. (Sir Jos.)
AND A LORD WHO RULES THE WATER –

SYBIL. (Josephine.) (*Aside.*)
AND A TAR WHO PLOUGHS THE WATER!
    ALL.
LET THE AIR WITH JOY BE LADEN,
REND WITH SONGS THE AIR ABOVE,
FOR THE UNION OF A MAIDEN
WITH THE MAN WHO OWNS HER LOVE!
    SYBIL. (Josephine.)
NEVER MIND THE WHY AND WHEREFORE,
LOVE CAN LEVEL RANKS, AND THEREFORE
I ADMIT THE JURISDICTION,
ABLY HAVE YOU PLAYED YOUR PART;
YOU HAVE CARRIED FIRM CONVICTION
TO MY HESITATING HEART.
RUTLAND. (Captain.) **& ALFRED.** (Sir Jos.)
RING THE MERRY BELLS ON BOARD-SHIP,
REND THE AIR WITH WARBLING WILD,
FOR THE UNION OF MY/HIS LORDSHIP
WITH A HUMBLE CAPTAIN'S CHILD!
    RUTLAND. (Captain.)
FOR A HUMBLE CAPTAIN'S DAUGHTER –
    SYBIL. (Josephine.)
FOR A GALLANT CAPTAIN'S DAUGHTER –
    ALFRED. (Sir Jos.)
AND A LORD WHO RULES THE WATER –
    SYBIL. (Josephine.)
AND A TAR WHO PLOUGHS THE WATER!
    ALL.
LET THE AIR WITH JOY BE LADEN,
REND WITH SONGS THE AIR ABOVE,
FOR THE UNION OF A MAIDEN
WITH THE MAN WHO OWNS HER LOVE!
    ALFRED. (Sir Jos.)
NEVER MIND THE WHY AND WHEREFORE,
LOVE CAN LEVEL RANKS, AND THEREFORE,
THOUGH YOUR NAUTICAL RELATION (*Alluding to Capt.*)
IN MY SET COULD SCARCELY PASS –

THOUGH YOU OCCUPY A STATION
IN THE LOWER MIDDLE CLASS –
    RUTLAND. (Captain.) & **ALFRED.** (Sir Jos.)
RING THE MERRY BELLS ON BOARD-SHIP,
REND THE AIR WITH WARBLING WILD,
FOR THE UNION OF MY/HIS LORDSHIP
WITH A HUMBLE CAPTAIN'S CHILD!
    RUTLAND. (Captain.)
FOR A HUMBLE CAPTAIN'S DAUGHTER –
    SYBIL. (Josephine.)
FOR A GALLANT CAPTAIN'S DAUGHTER –
    ALFRED. (Sir Jos.)
AND A LORD WHO RULES THE WATER –
    SYBIL. (Josephine.) (*Aside.*)
AND A TAR WHO PLOUGHS THE WATER –
    RUTLAND. (Captain.) & **ALFRED.** (Sir Jos.)
LET THE AIR WITH JOY BE LADEN,
RING THE MERRY BELLS ON BOARD-SHIP –
    SYBIL. (Josephine.)
FOR THE UNION OF A MAIDEN
    RUTLAND. (Captain.) & **ALFRED.** (Sir Jos.)
FOR HER UNION WITH HIS/MY LORDSHIP.
REND WITH SONGS THE AIR ABOVE
    ALL.
FOR THE MAN WHO OWNS HER LOVE!

(*As the music ends, ALFRED roars with delight – "Ha-haah!" – and grabs SYBIL and RUTLAND, hugging them gratefully. Before GILBERT, who is on his feet, can say anything, ALFRED breaks from the others and rushes at GILBERT. He almost hugs him, too, but stops abruptly a foot in front of him, realizing that one does not hug GILBERT. Instead, filled with excited energy, he jumps up and down with delight. GILBERT is speechless.*)

[MUSIC CUE #19: (NEVER MIND TAG)]

Scene 2

Gilbert and Sullivan's dressing room. A few minutes later.

The room is empty. After a moment, the door opens and KITTY appears. She looks around the room, sees that it's empty, then leads in SULLIVAN.)

KITTY. He's not here.

SULLIVAN. Good.

KITTY. I'll go find him. You just sit down and wait for me.

SULLIVAN. I don't like it. I shouldn't be here.

KITTY. Arthur, you deserve an apology and you're going to get one.

SULLIVAN. I think I should go –

KITTY. Arthur, sit down! (*He does.*) Now promise me you will not leave here until I find William. (*No response.*) Promise me.

SULLIVAN. Oh all right.

KITTY. Read something. I'll be right back. (*She leaves the room, closing the door behind her.*)

(SULLIVAN paces for a moment, hangs up his coat and hat, moves Gilbert's ottoman to his own chair, then sits down, wondering what to do with himself. A few seconds later, the door opens and GILBERT enters.

Both men are startled: GILBERT expected to find no one, least of all SULLIVAN; SULLIVAN expected KITTY. At first sight, they begin to say something, but catch themselves. Neither wants to be the first to speak. Instead they just stare angrily at each other. Then GILBERT shakes his head deprecatingly and SULLIVAN looks away.

The next minute or so is entirely pantomimed. GILBERT walks to the liquor table and pours himself a drink. Meanwhile SULLIVAN spies a newspaper, picks it up, chooses a section, then tosses the other section on the ottoman; GILBERT ignoring him, puts his drink on the table next to his chair, then walks towards SULLIVAN. SULLIVAN raises his leg to put his foot on the ottoman, when GILBERT snatches it, along with the newspaper, and returns it to its usual position in front of his own chair. GILBERT sits, puts his foot up on the ottoman and begins reading the paper. Both men sit there, reading, their faces obscured by the newspapers. Several seconds pass. Then SULLIVAN turns a page, snapping the paper as he does so. Pause. GILBERT turns a page with a similar snap. GILBERT turns a page – snap. Pause. Snap. Pause. Snap. The turning and snapping accelerate until both men throw their papers to the floor (or tear them to shreds) and jump up. GILBERT roars "Dammit, Sullivan!" – just as KITTY enters at the door left.)

KITTY. (*To GILBERT.*) There you are!
GILBERT. Kitty! What are you doing here?
KITTY. I want you to apologize to Arthur this minute.
GILBERT. So that's it. Ran to Mummy, did you?
SULLIVAN. Kitty, I'm leaving ...
KITTY. (*To SULLIVAN.*) Stay where you are. William, Arthur came to see me, as well he should, and I am outraged. At both of you. This display is totally uncalled for.
SULLIVAN. Kitty –
GILBERT. Kitty, you don't know the facts.
SULLIVAN. She knows the facts! Thanks to you.
GILBERT. I was trying to help him!
KITTY. William, pipe down!

(SULLIVAN turns away with a smile at this rebuke.)

KITTY. Arthur, turn around.

GILBERT. The girl is wrong for him, Kitty. I know she is —

SULLIVAN. You do not!

GILBERT. Of course I do!

KITTY. How do you know? Just how do you know, William?! You have been wrong before!

GILBERT. (*Embarrassed.*) Kitty, I told you ...

KITTY. So you did.

SULLIVAN. He's embarrassed now.

GILBERT. I am not!

SULLIVAN. You are so!

GILBERT. I saw her!

SULLIVAN. So what!

GILBERT. With my own eyes!

KITTY. Stop it *both* of you! (*Pause.*) You should be ashamed of yourselves.

GILBERT. Kitty, believe me, I didn't do anything —

SULLIVAN. Oh, you should have heard what he said—

GILBERT. The girl has a past, she'll make him miserable —

KITTY. William! I am sure if Arthur picked her, she must be lovely.

SULLIVAN. Thank you, my dear.

GILBERT. I was trying to help.

SULLIVAN. Some help.

GILBERT. All right, fine. Fine. Just do as you please.

SULLIVAN. I will, thank you.

KITTY. Come here. Both of you.

GILBERT. What do you want?

KITTY. Come *here!* (*They do.*) Now shake hands.

SULLIVAN. Never!

GILBERT. (*Simultaneously.*) Ha!

SULLIVAN. He hasn't apologized.

GILBERT. Oh, sure.

KITTY. (*To SULLIVAN.*) William is sorry. Believe me, I can tell. Now shake hands!

SULLIVAN. (*Pause.*) I'm willing. If he takes it
back...
GILBERT. Me? You're the one who got personal.
SULLIVAN. *I* got personal!? Oh my God – !
GILBERT. (*Overlapping.*) "Ridiculous rhymes" –
KITTY. Not another WORD! Let's go!

(*Finally, reluctantly, without looking at each other, they
shake hands.*)

KITTY. There. And now you feel better. (*To
GILBERT –*) Don't you?
GILBERT. Peachy.
KITTY. Now both of you, together – "I'm sorry."
GILBERT. Oh for heaven's sake –
SULLIVAN. (*Simultaneously.*) Kitty –
KITTY. Come on!

(*Another pause. They both mumble: "Sorry." "Sorry."*)

KITTY. (*Sighs.*) Now that's over.
GILBERT. (*Mumbles.*) Peachy ...
SULLIVAN. (*Mumbles.*) Over ...
KITTY. And let's keep it that way.
GILBERT. (*Mumbles.*) Oh yes ...
SULLIVAN. (*Mumbles.*) With him ...
KITTY. Can I trust you two? Alone? Is that possible?
GILBERT. Yes, yes. You can leave now.
KITTY. Good. (*To GILBERT.*) Five pounds, please.
GILBERT. Five – ? What for?!
KITTY. Dinner and my hair.
GILBERT. You have hair.
SULLIVAN. (*Reaching for his wallet.*) I can give it to
you ...
GILBERT. I have it! (*He hands her the money.*) Here.
KITTY. Thank you. I'll see you both later. Just don't
try anything while I'm gone. Agreed?
GILBERT. (*Mumbles.*) "Agreed?"

SULLIVAN. (*Mumbles.*) Yes ...

(*KITTY takes a last look at them, shakes her head and exits.*
Pause. They avoid each other's eyes.)

SULLIVAN. (*Finally.*) How you ever got that wonderful woman to marry you, I will never know.
GILBERT. She was too young to know better.

(*The tension eases slightly. GILBERT retrieves his glass, then goes to the liquor table and makes two fresh drinks. Meanwhile SULLIVAN picks up the newspapers and straightens them. Longish pause. GILBERT hands SULLIVAN his drink.*)

SULLIVAN. Thank you.
GILBERT. Cheers.
SULLIVAN. Cheers.
GILBERT. To the show.
SULLIVAN. It will be all right? ...
GILBERT. Fine.
SULLIVAN. I mean, Alfred? ...
GILBERT. Yes, yes. (*He hobbles to his chair and sits.*) I spent some time with him this afternoon. He is not what I would call a quick study.
SULLIVAN. No. (*Pause.*) I do appreciate it.
GILBERT. Not at all. (*Pause.*) Perhaps some day I shall want my cat to appear ... (*Pause.*) in *Ivanhoe.*

(*They look at each other. The lights fade.*)

[MUSIC CUE #20: TRANSITION TO SCENE 3]

Scene 3

The Savoy stage. A few minutes later.
The SAVOYARDS are relaxing onstage having a tea
break. GEORGE and VIOLET enter from the wings.
She has a distressed look on her face as he ushers her
onstage by the arm.

GEORGE. Now don't worry, my dear. You'll be just
fine.
VIOLET. Sir Arthur promised to rehearse it with me.
And I can't find him anywhere.
GEORGE. This is very unlike him.
VIOLET. Are you sure you don't mind? It's very kind
of you.
GEORGE. (*Flattered.*) Of course not, my dear. Now
just relax. (*Peering into the pit –*) Cellier? Ah. If you
don't mind, we'd like to run through our duet. *Ruddigore.*
Number twenty-two, I think.
VIOLET. (*To GEORGE.*) I don't want to let you down.
GEORGE. That's impossible. Cellier?
CELLIER. It's not on the schedule, George.
GEORGE. I know that, old boy. But, you see, Miss
Russell and I would like to rehearse it. (*To VIOLET.*)
Now, you stand here ... Turn just a little ...
CELLIER. Gilbert won't like it, George.
GEORGE. I'll take care of him. Just play the song,
thank you.

(CELLIER hesitates, mutters something and turns to the
music.)

GEORGE. (*To VIOLET.*) There, now head up,
shoulders back, and do it all from here. (*T h e*
diaphragm.) All right?
VIOLET. All right. Ahem.

(They stand still, ready to sing. Longish pause.)

CELLIER. George, why don't we ask him?
GEORGE. Will you play the song! I will take full responsibility. You have my word as a gentleman.

[MUSIC CUE #21: I KNOW A YOUTH]

(CELLIER shrugs and begins the introduction to "I Know a Youth Who Loves a Little Maid" from Ruddigore. GEORGE, as Robin Oakapple, and VIOLET as Rose Maybud, sing the love song straight through. During the song, ALFRED enters and ROSINA stands, gazing at him with rapture. ALFRED's attention is fixed on VIOLET.)

SONG (Duet)
GEORGE. (Robin.)
I KNOW A YOUTH WHO LOVES A LITTLE MAID–
(HEY, BUT HIS FACE IS A SIGHT FOR TO SEE!)
SILENT IS HE, FOR HE'S MODEST AND AFRAID –
(HEY, BUT HE'S TIMID AS A YOUTH CAN BE!)
VIOLET. (Rose.)
I KNOW A MAID WHO LOVES A GALLANT YOUTH,
(HEY, BUT SHE SICKENS AS THE DAYS GO BY!)
SHE CANNOT TELL HIM ALL THE SAD, SAD TRUTH–
(HEY, BUT I THINK THAT LITTLE MAID WILL DIE!)
GEORGE. (Robin.)
POOR LITTLE MAN!
VIOLET. (Rose.)
POOR LITTLE MAID!
GEORGE. ((Robin.)
POOR LITTLE MAN!
VIOLET. (ROSE.)
POOR LITTLE MAID!
BOTH.
NOW TELL ME PRAY, AND TELL ME TRUE,

WHAT IN THE WORLD SHOULD THE YOUNG
MAN/MAIDEN DO?
GEORGE. (Robin.)
HE CANNOT EAT AND HE CANNOT SLEEP
(HEY, BUT HIS FACE IS A SIGHT FOR TO SEE!)
DAILY HE GOES FOR TO WAIL – FOR TO WEEP
(HEY, BUT HE'S WRETCHED AS A YOUTH CAN BE!)
VIOLET. (Rose.)
SHE'S VERY THIN AND SHE'S VERY PALE
(HEY, BUT SHE SICKENS AS THE DAYS GO BY!)
DAILY SHE GOES FOR TO WEEP – FOR TO WAIL–
(HEY, BUT I THINK THAT LITTLE MAID WILL DIE!)
GEORGE. (Robin.)
POOR LITTLE MAID!
VIOLET. (Rose.)
POOR LITTLE MAN!
GEORGE. (Robin.)
POOR LITTLE MAID!
VIOLET. (Rose.)
POOR LITTLE MAN!
BOTH.
NOW TELL ME PRAY, AND TELL ME TRUE,
WHAT IN THE WORLD SHOULD THE YOUNG
MAN/MAIDEN DO?
VIOLET. (Rose.)
IF I WERE THE YOUTH I SHOULD OFFER HER MY
NAME –
(HEY, BUT HER FACE IS A SIGHT FOR TO SEE!)
GEORGE. (Robin.)
IF I WERE THE MAID I SHOULD FAN HIS HONEST
FLAME
(HEY, BUT HE'S BASHFUL AS A YOUTH CAN BE!)
VIOLET. (Rose.)
IF I WERE THE YOUTH I SHOULD SPEAK TO HER
TO-DAY.
(HEY, BUT SHE SICKENS AS THE DAYS GO BY!)

GEORGE. (Robin.)
IF I WERE THE MAID I SHOULD MEET THE LAD
    HALF WAY –
(FOR I REALLY DO BELIEVE THAT TIMID YOUTH
    WILL DIE!)
VIOLET. (Rose.)
POOR LITTLE MAN!
GEORGE. (Robin.)
POOR LITTLE MAID!
VIOLET. (Rose.)
POOR LITTLE MAN!
GEORGE. (Robin.)
POOR LITTLE MAID!
BOTH.
I THANK YOU, MISS/SIR, FOR YOUR COUNSEL
    TRUE,
I'LL TELL THAT YOUTH/MAID WHAT HE/SHE
    OUGHT TO DO!

(As soon as the song is over ALFRED jumps up, clapping enthusiastically.)

ALFRED. Brava! Brava! *(He rushes to VIOLET.)* It was ravishing, my dear, simply ravishing!
GEORGE. Very nice indeed. You have nothing to worry about.
VIOLET. Thank you so much. I feel much better. *(She kisses GEORGE on the cheek.)*

(By this time CARTE, trailed by GILBERT and SULLIVAN, has entered from the wings.)

CARTE. Now what the devil is going on here?! That song does not appear on my schedule! Miss Russell –
GILBERT. *(Stopping him.)* Carte. Just forget about it.
CARTE. But William –
GILBERT. Carte – !

GEORGE. Now don't blame her, Richard. It's not her fault. (*Beat.*) It was Cellier's idea.
CELLIER. *George!*
GILBERT. Rutland!
RUTLAND. Here!

(*As GILBERT continues, SULLIVAN draws VIOLET aside and they talk quietly. Also, during the following, DURWARD and COURTICE drift in from the wings.*)

GILBERT. George! Let's go! Look at the time!
GEORGE. All set.
GILBERT. Now let's get it right, shall we? Sullivan!
SULLIVAN. Watching!
GILBERT. Lights!

[MUSIC CUE #22A-D: WHEN I GO OUT OF DOOR]

(*CELLIER begins the light, bouncy introduction to "When I Go Out of Door" from Patience. The introduction consists of an ascending triplet phrase repeated over and over; the phrase is not only increasingly distinctive, but unaccountably catchy – it calls out to the be danced to. It leads directly to the Bunthorne/GEORGE - Grosvenor/RUTLAND due. Bunthorne's prop is a monocle; Grosvenor's prop is a walking stick.*)

<u>SONG</u>
GEORGE. (Bun.)
WHEN I GO OUT OF DOOR,
OF DAMOZELS A SCORE
(ALL SIGHING AND BURNING
AND CLINGING AND YEARNING)
WILL FOLLOW ME AS BEFORE.
GILBERT. (*Overlapping.*) Hold it! Stop! STOP! (*The music halts feebly.*) It's all wrong. You've got to think!

This is Bunthorne. Full of life! He's a poet, not an undertaker. It's got to be smooth and satisfied.

GEORGE. (*A bit peeved.*) Sorry.

GILBERT. Let's try Rutland. First solo.

(*The same musical introduction. RUTLAND shoots GEORGE a skeptical glance.*)

SONG

RUTLAND. (Grosv.)
CONCEIVE ME IF YOU CAN
AN EVERY-DAY YOUNG MAN:
A COMMONPLACE TYPE,
WITH A STICK AND A PIPE,

GILBERT. (*Overlapping.*) No no no! (*The music halts. RUTLAND sighs.*) It's all lumpy. "Conceive me *if* you *can.*" It's not a march, for God's sake.

RUTLAND. Yes, but I thought in contrast to Bunthorne ...

GILBERT. (*Impatiently, but not unkindly.*) Well that's true. But it's there already, in the words. I mean, you used to do it. (*Slightly confused –*) It just sounds funny ...

SULLIVAN. (*From the sidelines.*) He's right, I'm afraid. It's a musical problem.

GILBERT. (*To the SINGERS.*) There. Musical problem. (*To SULLIVAN.*) Explain it to them.

SULLIVAN. (*To the SINGERS.*) Well, it's just the same old thing, really. You're singing it in 4/4 time. But, as you know, it's in 6/8, which changes the phrase. "*One* two, *one* two ... Conceive me if you *can*, a *matter* of fact young *man* ..."

GILBERT. That's it! And you've got to move with it. Smoothly. (*Dancing –*) "When I got out of door, Of damozels a score –"

SULLIVAN. (*Overlapping.*) *One* two, *one* two –

GILBERT. Let's try it, together. (*To CELLIER –*) Hold the orchestra. (*Singing the introduction –*) *Da* da da, da da da, *Da* da da, first verse, *Da* da da, da da da, *Da* da da, da –

GILBERT, SULLIVAN, GEORGE & RUTLAND.
(*Singing a capella and dancing.*)
WHEN I GO OUT OF DOOR,
OF DAMOZELS A SCORE
(ALL SIGHING AND BURNING,
AND CLINGING AND YEARNING)
WILL FOLLOW ME AS BEFORE.
      SULLIVAN. Better!
      GILBERT, SULLIVAN, GEORGE & RUTLAND.
I SHALL WITH CULTURED TASTE,
DISTINGUISH GEMS FROM PASTE,
      GILBERT. That's it!
      GILBERT, SULLIVAN, GEORGE & RUTLAND.
AND "HIGH DIDDLE DIDDLE"
WILL RANK AS AN IDYLL,
IF I PRONOUNCE IT CHASTE!

(*The CAST MEMBERS onstage burst into applause.
"Hear hear! "Keep it up!"*)

      SULLIVAN. That's it.
      GILBERT. Much better.
      RUTLAND. I see ...
      SULLIVAN. (*Still dancing.*) da *Da* da da da *da* ...
(*Etc.*)
      GILBERT. (*Joining him.*) It's all in the feet ... *One*,
two, *one*, two ... (*Etc.*)

(*At this moment CELLIER gets a bright idea. He begins
playing the introduction – the triplet phrase that we
now recognize.*)

      GILBERT. (*To CELLIER.*) Not yet!

(*But CELLIER ignores GILBERT and the phrase
continues. Because it's circular, it can go on forever.*)

GILBERT. Cellier! ...
CELLIER. Go ahead!
GILBERT. Very funny.

(*But the phrase continues ...*)

GILBERT. Cellier ...
SULLIVAN. Don't be silly ...

(*The phrase goes on ... And now the idea travels through the CAST MEMBERS onstage, who begin to clap in time to the music.*)

JESSIE. Come on boys. Do it up!
ROSINA. Sing it, Billy!
SYBIL. "From the top, please!"
RUTLAND. (*Imitating GILBERT.*) "Lights!"

(*Laughing, the CAST continue to clap with the music — and then they begin stamping their feet.*)

GILBERT. Don't be ridiculous.
SULLIVAN. Gilbert ...
JESSIE. (*Above the rest.*) Scaredy-cats!
SULLIVAN. Jessie! ...

(*But on it goes, the phrase and the clapping, with more and more hoots from the CAST –*)

DURWARD. And now –
COURTICE. Presenting –
ROSINA. Straight from Hounslow –
ALL. Gilbert *and* Sullivan! (*Cheers.*)

(*RUTLAND ceremoniously presents his walking stick to GILBERT; and GEORGE presents his monocle to SULLIVAN. GILBERT and SULLIVAN give up.*)

SULLIVAN. (*To GILBERT.*) Grosvenor?
GILBERT. (*To SULLIVAN.*) Bunthorne?

(*A deep breath – and they begin the song, GILBERT playing Grosvenor and SULLIVAN, Bunthorne. Singing, dancing, even clowning, they perform the duet from beginning to end.*)

SONG (Duet)
SULLIVAN. (Bun.)
WHEN I GO OUT OF DOOR,
OF DAMOZELS A SCORE
(ALL SIGHING AND BURNING,
AND CLINGING AND YEARNING)
WILL FOLLOW ME AS BEFORE.
I SHALL, WITH CULTURED TASTE,
DISTINGUISH GEMS FROM PASTE,
AND "HIGH DIDDLE DIDDLE"
WILL RANK AS AN IDYLL,
IF I PRONOUNCE IT CHASTE!
    BOTH.
A MOST INTENSE YOUNG MAN,
A SOULFUL-EYED YOUNG MAN,
AN ULTRA-POETICAL, SUPER-AESTHETICAL,
OUT-OF-THE-WAY YOUNG MAN!
    GILBERT. (Grosv.)
CONCEIVE ME, IF YOU CAN,
AN EVERY-DAY YOUNG MAN;
A COMMONPLACE TYPE,
WITH A STICK AND A PIPE,
AND A HALF-BRED BLACK-AND-TAN;
WHO THINKS SUBURBAN "HOPS"
MORE FUN THAN "MONDAY POPS,"
WHO'S FOND OF HIS DINNER,
AND DOESN'T GET THINNER
ON BOTTLED BEER AND CHOPS.

BOTH.
A COMMONPLACE YOUNG MAN,
A MATTER-OF-FACT YOUNG MAN,
A STEADY AND STOLID-Y, JOLLY
BANK-HOLIDAY
EVERY-DAY YOUNG MAN!
    SULLIVAN. (Bun.)
A JAPANESE YOUNG MAN,
A BLUE-AND-WHITE YOUNG MAN,
FRANCESCA DA RIMINI, MIMINY, PIMINY,
JE-NE-SAIS-QUOI YOUNG MAN!
    GILBERT. (Grosv.)
A CHANCERY LANE YOUNG MAN,
A SOMERSET HOUSE YOUNG MAN,
A VERY DELECTABLE, HIGHLY RESPECTABLE,
THREEPENNY-BUS YOUNG MAN!
    SULLIVAN. (Bun.)
A PALLID AND THIN YOUNG MAN,
A HAGGARD AND LANK YOUNG MAN,
A GREENERY-YALLERY, GROSVENOR GALLERY,
FOOT-IN-THE-GRAVE YOUNG MAN!
    GILBERT. (Grosv.)
A SEWELL & CROSS YOUNG MAN,
A HOWELL & JAMES YOUNG MAN,
A PUSHING YOUNG PARTICLE –
"WHAT'S THE NEXT ARTICLE?" –
WATERLOO-HOUSE YOUNG MAN!

<u>Ensemble</u>

SULLIVAN. (Bun.)	**GILBERT.** (Grosv.)
CONCEIVE ME, IF YOU CAN,	CONCEIVE ME, IF YOU CAN,
A CROTCHETY, CRACKED YOUNG MAN,	A MATTER-OF-FACT YOUNG MAN,

AN ULTRA-
 POETICAL,
 SUPER-
 AESTHETICAL,
OUT-OF-THE-WAY
 YOUNG MAN!

AN ALPHABETICAL,
 ARITHMETICAL,

EVERY-DAY YOUNG
 MAN!

(Sustained applause and cheers from the CAST. Then CELLIER begins the introduction again, a half-step higher.)

GILBERT. Cellier!

(But the CAST are insistent, and they sing a reprise.)

REPRISE[*]
SULLIVAN. (Bun.)
A MAN WHOM GIRLS ADMIRE,
FOR RENAISSANCE ATTIRE,
THEY FIGHT FOR A SCRAP
OF MY RHYTHMICAL PAP
AND IT SETS THEIR HEARTS ON FIRE.
   GILBERT. (Grosv.)
A MAN WHO LIKES HIS TEA,
A BLANKET ON HIS KNEE
A MAN OF LONG FACES
WITHOUT ANY TRACES
OF IMMORALITY.
   SULLIVAN. (Bun.)
A LONGISH HAIR YOUNG MAN,
A NOSE-IN-THE-AIR YOUNG MAN,
A QUITE UNMISTAKABLE
EASILY BREAKABLE

---

[*] The lyrics to the Reprise, except for the first four lines of the Ensemble, are the property of the author, Copyright 1982 by Ken Ludwig.

CULTURED AND RARE YOUNG MAN.
    GILBERT. (Grosv.)
A FISTICUFF YOUNG MAN,
A BRAWNY BLUFF YOUNG MAN,
A LOVER OF BATTLE-ING
TITTLE-ING TATTLE-ING
COUNTRY-STUFF YOUNG MAN.
    SULLIVAN. (Bun.)
A FINE ELITE YOUNG MAN,
AN INDISCREET YOUNG MAN,
A SIT-IN-THE-PRIORY
WRITING HIS DIARY
CHARMING EFFETE YOUNG MAN.
    GILBERT. (Grosv.)
A CASH-IN-THE-BANK YOUNG MAN,
A TERRIBLY FRANK YOUNG MAN,
A HIGHLY PERSNICKETY
TENDING TO RICKETY
PAIN-IN-THE-FLANK YOUNG MAN.

<u>Ensemble</u>

SULLIVAN. (Bun.)	**GILBERT.** (Grosv.)
CONCEIVE ME, IF YOU CAN,	CONCEIVE ME, IF YOU CAN,
A CROTCHETY, CRACKED YOUNG MAN,	A MATTER-OF-FACT YOUNG MAN,
AN ULTRA-POETICAL, SUPER-AESTHETICAL,	AN ALPHABETICAL, ARITHMETICAL,
OUT-OF-THE-WAY YOUNG MAN!	EVERY-DAY YOUNG MAN!
CONCEIVE ME, IF YOU CAN,	CONCEIVE ME, IF YOU CAN,

A CROTCHETY,   A MATTER-OF-FACT
    CRACKED   YOUNG MAN,
    YOUNG MAN,
    SULLIVAN. (Bun.)
MOZART AND ROSSINI-EST,
TEENIEST WEENIEST –
    GILBERT. (Grosv.)
A NOT-SO-RELIGIOUS,
BUT HIGHLY LITIGIOUS –
    SULLIVAN. (Bun.)
TSCHAIKOVSKY AND HANDEL
DON'T HOLD UP A CANDLE –
    GILBERT. (Grosv.)
A GRUFF AND DIDACTICAL,
PLEASINGLY PRACTICAL –
    SULLIVAN. (Bun.)
LIKE BACH AND BEETHOVEN,
THE TWO INTERWOVEN –
    GILBERT. (Grosv.)
A MAN WHO CAN STICK IT
THROUGH TWO GAMES OF CRICKET –
    SULLIVAN. (Bun.)
A TRULY SENSATIONAL
QUITE INSPIRATIONAL –
    GILBERT. (Grosv.)
WITH TWO ACHING FEET
THAT ARE NOW OBSOLETE –

    <u>Ensemble</u>
    SULLIVAN. (Bun.)   **GILBERT.**
                                  (Grosv.)

AN ULTRA-   AN ALPHABETICAL,
    POETICAL,   ARITHMETICAL,
    SUPER-
    AESTHETICAL,
OUT-OF-THE-WA-A-   EVERY-DA-A-AY
    AY YOUNG MAN!   YOUNG MAN!

(The CAST burst into applause.)

SULLIVAN. *(Aside to GILBERT.)* Well done.
GILBERT. *(To GEORGE and RUTLAND.)* You get the idea.

(CARTE bustles across the stage, clipboard in hand, calling out –)

CARTE. That's it! Clear the stage!
SULLIVAN. Not already?
GILBERT. Carte ...
CARTE. Forget it. Time's up.
GILBERT. *(Checking his watch.)* Carte –
CARTE. *(Shouting to the balcony.)* PRIMROSE!?
SULLIVAN. Richard. I think we'd like to say a few words ...
CARTE. Oh. Sorry. *(To the CAST –)* Over here. Sit down, sit down ... *(Reading from his clipboard and ticking off the names with a pencil as the cast gather into a group.)* Barrington. ("Here!") Bond. ("Here!") Brandram. ("Here!") Grey. ("Here!") Grossmith. ("Here!") Lely. ("Here!") Pounds. ("Here!") Russell. ("Here!") *(Pause.)* And His Royal Highness.
ALFRED. Here!
CARTE. That's the lot. *(To GILBERT and SULLIVAN.)* All right, who's first?
GILBERT. *(To SULLIVAN.)* After you.
SULLIVAN. *(To GILBERT.)* Please.
GILBERT. *(To SULLIVAN.)* Go ahead.

(A hush descends as the CAST wait for their opening-night speeches. Pause.)

SULLIVAN. *(Addressing the CAST.)* Well – here we are. Eleven shows later.
GILBERT. *(Mutters.)* Ruddigore.

SULLIVAN. Twelve shows later. (*Pause. Slowly with increasing conviction.*) We have certainly been through a great deal together, good and bad. Most of it good. I look at all of you and I think how the happiest moments of my life have been spent with you here, under the lights, where none of us grows older. With Jessie, ripping three costumes on the same night. (*Laughter.*) With Rosina, who one fine day just happened to leave the only score to *Penzance* in a hackney cab in the middle of New York City. (*Laughter.*) With George, his first night on a professional stage. *The Sorcerer.* Do you remember, George? We held him together with a pair of suspenders and a large glass of brandy. (*Laughter.*) With all of you at different times, helping me, helping us, (*Indicating GILBERT.*), helping each other, and always, always giving nothing but the very best for the good of the show. Tonight we face yet another milestone, our first revue, and to make matters worse, we have a Queen to please. If it makes you nervous, don't worry, it has me petrified. But no matter what happens, this much I do know – that no more loyal cast was ever assembled on one stage in the history of the English theatre. And ... I hope you don't mind if I think of you all, not just as singers and actors, of which you are the very best, but as my own family, for I love you all. God bless you and good luck. (*Greatly moved, he is forced to look away.*)
        CARTE. William.
        GILBERT. (*To SULLIVAN.*) Thanks a lot.

(*Again the CAST settle in.*)

        GILBERT. Needless to say, I agree with every word of my distinguished colleague. If you weren't the cream, you wouldn't be here; and if you weren't nervous, you'd be dead. Let me only remind you that tonight, fully nineteen years after we started this madness, you will be singing before the Queen of England, perhaps the finest tribute that will ever be paid to you. Under these circumstances, I

urge you to think what a pleasure it would be ... if we
could all HEAR THE WORDS for a change. (*Laughter.
Relief.*) Curtain at eight!
     CARTE. And places at seven-fifty!

(*The CAST rise, mingle, disperse, all chatting and
     laughing.*)

     CARTE. (*To GILBERT and SULLIVAN.*) Well,
gentlemen, would you like some dinner?
     SULLIVAN. Hm? ... Oh. No, I don't think so.
Nervous tummy.
     GILBERT. I know what you mean.
     CARTE. Nothing?
     GILBERT. Well ... Soup, I guess. Pork chops. Fried
potatoes, Green salad. Pudding.
     SULLIVAN. (*A bit green.*) Excuse me.
     CARTE. (*Also green.*) Excuse me.

(*They exit. GILBERT looks at them curiously and exits
     after them.*)

          [MUSIC CUE #23: TRANSITION TO SCENE 4]

                         Scene 4

The Savoy Stage. Immediately following.
*Most of the cast are gone now, and the stage is shadowed
     in working lights. After a few more seconds, only
     ALFRED and VIOLET are left onstage. VIOLET is
     sitting alone, taking in the empty theatre. ALFRED
     hesitates, then walks up to her.*

     ALFRED. Well – this is it.
     VIOLET. This is it. Break a leg.
     ALFRED. Hm?

VIOLET. Break a leg.

ALFRED. What for?

VIOLET. That means good luck. In the theatre.

ALFRED. It does? How charming. Break a leg ...

ALFRED. (*Pause.*) Are you nervous?

VIOLET. A little. Are you?

ALFRED. I'm in shock. My hands are like little icebergs.

(*She takes his hands for a moment.*)

VIOLET. You poor thing. You're frozen!

ALFRED. I told you.

VIOLET. Now don't worry.

ALFRED. If I fluff up, I'll just kill myself.

VIOLET. Don't do that. (*Pause.*) I'd miss you.

ALFRED. Would you really?

VIOLET. I'm afraid so.

ALFRED. Of course, I will see you again. I mean, I won't be here every night, but I can stop by. I mean, I will stop by.

VIOLET. (*Looking at him.*) I hope so.

ALFRED. (*Pause.*) Perhaps I'll give a party. For the entire cast. What do you think?

VIOLET. I'd love it.

ALFRED. (*Excitedly.*) Sort of "thank you" to everyone. Nothing formal. Maybe at Windsor, if Mama's not using it. You would come?

VIOLET. I wouldn't miss it for the world.

ALFRED. Do you promise?

VIOLET. Cross my heart.

(*At this moment SULLIVAN enters from the wings; he sees them almost immediately and stops short. He hesitates, then withdraws into the shadows, watching them. They have no idea that he's there, and their conversation continues without interruption.*)

ALFRED. Let's say next Sunday, then. You tell the girls, I'll tell the boys. My God, we'll have fun! Do you think they'll come?

VIOLET. I'm sure they will.

ALFRED. Nothing fancy, sort of picnic style. And we can stuff ourselves.

VIOLET. I will.

ALFRED. So will I!

VIOLET. (*Pause.*) We'd better be going.

ALFRED. Right. I will see you ...?

VIOLET. I promise.

(*They both hesitate. Then, slowly, gently, they kiss. When it ends, ALFRED is surprised and embarrassed.*)

ALFRED. Sorry. Stupid of me.

VIOLET. Not at all.

ALFRED. I don't know, uh, why ...

VIOLET. It's all right.

ALFRED. (*Pause.*) Well ... break your leg.

VIOLET. (*Fondly.*) You too.

(*They turn to exit in opposite directions. ALFRED disappears. VIOLET is almost off when she sees SULLIVAN.*)

VIOLET. Arthur!

SULLIVAN. I'm just going ...

VIOLET. Arthur, wait ... (*He stops.*) Let me say something.

SULLIVAN. There's nothing to say. I didn't see anything.

VIOLET. Arthur ...

SULLIVAN. I didn't *see* it!

VIOLET. (*Pause.*) He kissed me. That's all.

SULLIVAN. He's married.

VIOLET. I know. It doesn't matter.

SULLIVAN. Because you ... love me?

VIOLET. I'm twenty-three, Arthur.

SULLIVAN. Twenty-three.

VIOLET. There's so much ... so much ... going on. I want to do it. *All* of it.

SULLIVAN. (*Stubbornly.*) I didn't see you kiss him.

VIOLET. It doesn't matter.

SULLIVAN. Of *course* it does —

VIOLET. No it *doesn't!* Don't you see? I can't live up to you. You know that. No matter what I do —

SULLIVAN. Of course you can —

VIOLET. There are *things*, Arthur. Certain things ... you don't know ...

SULLIVAN. I don't care.

VIOLET. You would care. You would care. Believe me.

SULLIVAN. I don't. I can't.

VIOLET. Believe me, Arthur. It wouldn't work. I need more time.

SULLIVAN. (*Pause.*) Which is the one thing I can't give you.

VIOLET. Oh, *Arthur!* ... (*Realizing what she's done, she breaks into tears.*) I'm sorry ... I'm ... I'm ... *sorry...*

SULLIVAN. (*Quietly.*) Don't be. (*Pause.*) It's getting late.

(*Impulsively she kisses him and runs from the stage. SULLIVAN watches her go, then stares blankly into the theatre as the lights fade.*)

[MUSIC CUE #24: BRIDGE TO SCENE 5]

Scene 5

A corridor backstage. An hour later.
GILBERT in white tie and tails, is pacing back and forth
    in front of a closed door – the door to his and
    SULLIVAN's dressing room. The corridor is empty
    except for a wardrobe basket (or trunk) along the back
    wall.
After a moment, KITTY and CARTE hurry on (dressed
    for opening night). Their dialogue with GILBERT is
    entirely in whispers.

KITTY. William!
CARTE. (*To GILBERT.*) Has he said anything?
GILBERT. Go away!
CARTE. Be we've only got twenty minutes –
KITTY. I know he'll listen to me –
GILBERT. (*To KITTY.*) How's the girl?
KITTY. Well I got her to stop crying at least. But I
can't get a word out of her.
GILBERT. Just as well ...
CARTE. I don't understand it – !
KITTY. William, perhaps if I spoke to him –
GILBERT. Kitty, please. Let me handle it.

(*At this point, GEORGE, RUTLAND and ROSINA hurry*
    on, distressed. They wear their costumes for "The
    Mikado" finale, but without their oriental wigs.)

GEORGE. William, this is awful!
GILBERT. Oh my God –!
ROSINA. (*To KITTY.*) How's Arthur?
KITTY. I don't know.
RUTLAND. We just heard.
ROSINA. Can we do anything?
GILBERT. You can get out!
CARTE. (*Calling out.*) Arthur?

GILBERT. Carte – !
CARTE. (*Calling out.*) Arthur, it's Richard.
GILBERT. Be quiet!
CARTE. William, I know if I spoke to him –
GILBERT. No you *don't* know!
CARTE. I'm telling you –
GILBERT. Do you want to *argue?!*
CARTE. (*Pause.*) Oh, all right.

(*GEORGE, RUTLAND and ROSINA exit, and KITTY and CARTE start out after them.*)

GILBERT. Carte. Tell Cellier to stand by.

(*CARTE moans and exits with KITTY.*
Again, GILBERT is alone with the door. When GILBERT finally speaks, he does it loudly, so that he can be heard through the door.)

GILBERT. I'm alone now, Sullivan. Just me. I promise. Now unlock the door. (*No response.*) Sullivan?!

(*Pause. No response.*)

GILBERT. Sullivan, listen to me. You're being irrational. The girl's upset. Extremely upset. It's clear she's fond of you. I don't know what happened. And I don't want to know. As you said, it's none of my business. Is it? Hm? (*No response.*) Look, I know it's a little late for this, but I do apologize. Really. I was wrong. No, not just because you're in there. I was *wrong*. The girl deserves to make a new start if she wants to. She's entitled. So I'm very sorry. (*No response.*) Perhaps if I write it down, hm? Yes ... (*He searches his pockets for a pencil and a scrap of paper; he finds them and begins to write.*) It means more in writing, I think. Here ... "Please accept my ... profound ... apology. Your ... friend, W.S. Gilbert." Schwenck. You can call me Schwenck, if you like. (*No *response.*) Now listen, Sullivan, I'm putting it under the door. Here it goes ... Now I'm leaving it sticking out this side, a little bit ... All right? Now – when it disappears, I'll know you've got it. Right? It's under now. (*Pause. The paper doesn't move.*) Sullivan? (*The paper remains. No response. Enraged, he suddenly rushes at the door and bangs at it.*) Let me in there this instant! Sullivan! (*No response. He breaks down.*) Arthur, don't abandon me! I am sorry, I am sorry, I am sorry.

(*GILBERT, unutterably sad and tired, turns and begins to leave. He's given up. He's almost gone when there's a noise at the door: the lock being unbolted. GILBERT turns. SULLIVAN emerges from the room. He's in white tie and tails. He sees on the floor the note that GILBERT wrote. He picks it up and puts it in his pocket without reading it. Pause.*)

SULLIVAN. It's not your fault.
GILBERT. I shouldn't meddle.
GILBERT. (*Pause.*) How are you feeling?
SULLIVAN. Fine.
GILBERT. With all the excitement –
SULLIVAN. I'm *fine*.
GILBERT. (*Pause.*) Drink?

(*SULLIVAN shakes his head no. They sit on the wardrobe basket. Pause. All is quiet.*)

GILBERT. I know it's a disappointment.
SULLIVAN. ... Yes.
GILBERT. It could have been worse. I mean – there's *Ivanhoe*. Think of that.
SULLIVAN. Junk.
GILBERT. Don't be modest.
SULLIVAN. Second-rate Verdi. Believe me.
GILBERT. Carte says it's brilliant. I'm sure it is. You might play me a bit of it – before it opens. A few bars.

Hm? (*No response.*) I'm sure that I will be very, very jealous of it. And of you. It's true. But Arthur, believe me ... I will be the first one on my feet at the curtain.

SULLIVAN. I know.

GILBERT. (*Pause.*) Of course you can't go by me. After all these years I can recognize only two songs. One is *God Save the Queen* –

GILBERT & SULLIVAN. (*Simultaneously.*) – and the other isn't.

GILBERT. You've heard that one. (*Pause.*) Will you conduct tonight? (*Gently.*) Arthur?

SULLIVAN. Yes. Of course. And we'll have curtain calls and good notices, telegrams and flowers. Business as usual.

GILBERT. It could be worse.

SULLIVAN. There is a certain comedy about us, William. Do you see it? Running here and there, changing the scenery, changing the costume. Morning coat, dinner coat. Scribbling, scribbling away, as if the more we scribble the more real we shall become. On and on. Don't you feel it?

GILBERT. No.

SULLIVAN. A great comedy, all around us, and we're the principals.

GILBERT. You and I?

SULLIVAN. All of us.

(*Pause. CARTE and KITTY hurry in.*)

CARTE. (*Off.*) Two minutes!
GILBERT. Right!
CARTE. ... Arthur!
KITTY. Arthur!
GILBERT. We will be there!

(*A cry of delight from KITTY, "Thank God!" from CARTE, and they exit.*)

GILBERT. (*Pause.*) Arthur ... Kitty and I have this friend. Name of Lottie Parks. We think the world of her, really —

SULLIVAN. William —

GILBERT. You may have met her actually. Reddish hair, good laugh — fine figure. Sort of Kitty's age, I'd say—

SULLIVAN. William — I don't want anyone else.

GILBERT. Choosy, choosy. But then you chose me, didn't you?

SULLIVAN. How very clever of me.

GILBERT. Come on.

SULLIVAN. Do I have to?

GILBERT. (*Hoarsely.*) Come *on.*

(*Slowly SULLIVAN rises. GILBERT looks at him, sighs with disgust and straightens Sullivan's tie.*
SULLIVAN pauses, takes Gilbert's note from his pocket and reads it to himself. Then he folds it, puts it back in his pocket and looks at GILBERT.)

SULLIVAN. Schwenck.

GILBERT. Let's go. We'll bring the house down.

(*They exit.*)

[MUSIC CUE #24A: ORCHESTRA TUNING]

Scene 6

A corridor backstage and the Savoy stage. Immediately following.
The back wall of the corridor is replaced with a scrim, and the lights are lowered, suggesting a backstage corridor that leads to the stage. Behind the scrim is the Savoy stage, shrouded in darkness.

(As SULLIVAN and GILBERT exit, the orchestra begins tuning up and the SAVOYARDS, in their Mikado costumes, begin hurrying through the corridor in the semi-darkness, whispering with excitement and nerves. They cross in front of the scrim, then go behind it and get into places for the opening number of their performance. When they're behind the scrim, we can see them in silhouette.)

RUTLAND. He's conducting!
SYBIL. We know!
JESSIE. We know!
COURTICE. How's the house?
DURWARD. It's packed.
RUTLAND. *(Jostled.)* Be careful!
COURTICE. I'm sorry!

(As this group heads behind the scrim, ROSINA and GEORGE enter, leading ALFRED, who's scared to death.)

ALFRED. I can't see a thing!
ROSINA. This way, your Royal Highness. This way.
GROSSMITH. You'll be fine. Don't worry.
ALFRED. I hope so.

(As they head behind the scrim, VIOLET enters alone and pauses halfway across the stage, unsure whether she can manage to go on. Simultaneously, we hear SYBIL and JESSIE behind the scrim –)

SYBIL. Vi?
JESSIE. Vi?
SYBIL. Where's Vi?
JESSIE. Violet?
VIOLET. *(Determined to go on.)* ... I'm right here.

(She dries her tears with the palm of her hand, then finishes the cross and joins the others behind the scrim. We see them all now in silhouette, hurrying into their opening positions.)

RUTLAND. Good luck!
COURTICE. Good show!
JESSIE. All the best!
DURWARD. Good luck!
SYBIL. Good luck!
ROSINA. All the best!
GROSSMITH. Good show!
ALFRED. Break your legs!

[MUSIC CUE #26: FINALE, PART I]

(Three chords from the orchestra, and as the scrim rises, the lights come up full to reveal the complete set for Act Two of "The Mikado.")

EPILOGUE

The Savoy stage. Immediately following.
As the lights come up, the COMPANY unfreezes. They sing the second verse of the "Madrigal" from The Mikado. The focus of the song is VIOLET, who dances in one direction, then another, trying to flee, but is stopped by each group of singers as they convey the advice of the song.

SONG
ALL.
LET US DRY THE READY TEAR,
THOUGH THE HOURS ARE SURELY CREEPING
LITTLE NEED FOR WOEFUL WEEPING,

TILL THE SAD SUNDOWN IS NEAR.
ALL MUST SIP THE CUP OF SORROW,
I TODAY AND THOU TOMORROW;
THIS THE CLOSE OF EVERY SONG –
DING DONG! DING DONG!
WHAT, THOUGH SOLEMN SHADOWS FALL,
SOONER, LATER, OVER ALL?
SING A MERRY MADRIGAL –
     A MADRIGAL!
 FAL-LA-FAL-LA!

(At the end of the song, the COMPANY freezes, suspended in time. Immediately, GILBERT and SULLIVAN step onto the stage, at opposite ends, each in his own pool of light. They address the audience.)

GILBERT. Gilbert
SULLIVAN. and Sullivan
GILBERT. wrote two more works together over the next six years. *Utopia Limited* and *The Grand Duke.*
SULLIVAN. In 1891, Sullivan's opera *Ivanhoe* opened at the Royal English Opera House. It was well-received, ran for six months, and was never heard of again.
GILBERT. Gilbert was not surprised.
SULLIVAN. Violet Russell eventually married and left the stage. Alfred returned to Marie of Russia, and there is no record of his ever appearing on the stage again. In 1900 Sullivan died, a confirmed old bachelor to the world around him. It was generally presumed that he had never loved.
GILBERT. Gilbert was knighted – finally – in 1907. He died four years later when he plunged into a lake to save a child from drowning. In the lonely years after Sullivan's death, Gilbert wrote the following note to Cellier: "A Gilbert is of no use without a Sullivan ... and I cannot find one!"

(GILBERT and SULLIVAN look at each other across the stage with irony and affection. Then they disappear into the wings as the COMPANY unfreezes and sings the "Mikado" finale.

In the finale, Pitti-Sing, Ko-Ko, Yum-Yum and Nanki-Poo are sung by JESSIE, GEORGE, VIOLET and DURWARD, respectively, with the rest of the CAST joining in the chorus.)

[MUSIC CUE #26A: FINALE, PART II]

JESSIE. (Pitti-Sing.)
FOR HE'S GONE AND MARRIED YUM-YUM –
    ALL.
YUM-YUM!
    JESSIE. (Pitti-Sing.)
YOUR ANGER PRAY BURY,
FOR ALL WILL BE MERRY,
I THINK YOU HAD BETTER SUCCUMB –
    ALL.
CUMB-CUMB!
    JESSIE. (Pitti-Sing.)
AND JOIN OUR EXPRESSIONS OF GLEE!
    GEORGE. (Ko-Ko)
ON THIS SUBJECT I PRAY YOU BE DUMB –
    ALL.
DUMB-DUMB!
    GEORGE. (Ko-Ko)
YOUR NOTIONS, THOUGH MANY,
ARE NOT WORTH A PENNY,
THE WORD FOR YOUR GUIDANCE IS "MUM" –
    ALL.
MUM-MUM!
    GEORGE. (Ko-Ko)
YOU'VE A VERY GOOD BARGAIN IN ME.
    ALL.
ON THIS SUBJECT WE PRAY YOU BE DUMB –
DUMB-DUMB!

WE THINK YOU HAD BETTER SUCCUMB –
CUMB-CUMB!
YOU'LL FIND THERE ARE MANY
WHO'LL WED FOR A PENNY,
THERE ARE LOTS OF GOOD FISH IN THE SEA.
    VIOLET & DURWARD. (Yum-Yum & Nanki-Poo)
THE THREATENED CLOUD HAS PASSED AWAY,
AND BRIGHTLY SHINES THE DAWNING DAY;
WHAT THOUGH THE NIGHT MAY COME TOO
    SOON,
WE'VE YEARS AND YEARS OF AFTERNOON!
    ALL.
THEN LET THE THRONG
OUR JOY ADVANCE,
WITH LAUGHING SONG
AND MERRY DANCE,
WITH JOYOUS SHOUT AND RINGING CHEER,
INAUGURATE OUR NEW CAREER! (*Etc.*)

(*Blackout.*)

CURTAIN

[MUSIC CUE # 27: BOWS]

COSTUME PRESET LIST

TOP OF SHOW PRESET:

STAGE RIGHT PROP TABLE:
Courtice Prop Costume (Green Velvet Waistcoat)

STAGE RIGHT QUICK CHANGE BOOTH:
Fat Suit (Rutland)
Full Tails (Sullivan)
Pirate Costume (Alfred)
- Shirt
- Skirt
- Jacket
- Shoes
- Scarf
- Hat
- Tights (Underdressed)
Fairy Wings and Harness (Rosina)

UPSTAGE OF DRESSING ROOM UNIT:
Pirate Belt (w/sword after Sc. 1)
Pirate Pistol

STAGE LEFT PROP TABLE:
Striped Skirt
Torn Corset

STAGE LEFT PROP TABLE:
3 Pink Academic Gowns
3 Drag Wigs w/hats attached
3 Academic Hats
White/Brown Nighty
Torn Skirt

ON STAGE LEFT DRESSING ROOM UNIT:
Mabel Costume
Rose Costume
Josephine Costume
Violet's Red Fake Kimono (2nd on rack)

STAGE LEFT QUICK CHANGE BOOTH(S):
Mikado Underwear: Jessie
Pitti-Sing Kimono: Jessie

Mikado Underwear: Sybil
Peep-Bo Kimono: Sybil

Mikado Underwear: Violet
Yum-Yum Kimono: Violet

Gentleman of Japan Trousers: Alfred
Tabi's (Socks): Alfred

Full Tails: Gilbert
Full Tails: Carte

STAGE LEFT MIKADO QUICK CHANGE AREA (FULL COSTUMES):
Ko-Ko Costume
Ko-Ko Wig

Pooh-Bah Costume
Pooh-Bah Wig

Pish-Tush Costume
Pish-Tush Wig

Nanki-Poo Costume
Nanki-Poo Wig

The Mikado Costume

The Mikado Wig

Gentleman of Japan Costume
Gentleman of Japan Wig

Katisha Costume
Katisha Wig

Pitti-Sing Costume
Pitti-Sing Wig

Peep-Bo Costume
Peep-Bo Wig

Yum-Yum Costume
Yum-Yum Wig

MASTER PROP LIST

Act One Prologue:
(Grim's Dyke - Sullivan)

Brown armchair (Gilbert SR); footstool (to match chair); oval occasional table w/gold ornate clock, brass ashtray, cigar box, ink well; potted palm and stand; canterbury w/newspapers; telephone; carpet on wagon.

(Queen's Mansion - Sullivan)

Green armchair (for Sullivan); square, tall occasional table w/ brass pot on legs, oriental vase on stand w/white flowers, oriental statue "man"; folding screen; small, square table; telephone w/ clicking arm; carpet on wagon; handled vase w/flowers.

Act One, Sc. 1:
(Savoy Stage)

Throat sprayer; make-up case (Violet); carpet bag w/wood handles (Sybil); cloth shopping bag (Jessie); *The Leader* newspaper (4 pages, 3rd page has picture of "Three Little Maids"; clipboard and papers (cast lists) w/pencil; clipboard and papers (schedules) w/pencil; sheet music (Rutland); 3 envelopes and 3 letters (mail) (Rutland); half a red apple; 2 spears; rack of costumes containing:

> 4 bobby hats
> 2 beefeaters' hats
> 2 beefeaters' uniforms on wooded hangers
> pirate costume bag
> filler hangers

Rack of costumes containing:

>9 prop costumes on wooden hangers
>3 wig blocks on top shelf
>5 hooks on end
>1 mirror on end
>1 ornate cane

Single lock skip w/sword in scabbard w/belt; double lock skip w/jester stick, hand mirror, tamborine, scroll; 1 upright piano; 4 bentwood chairs; 2 prop pinrails; 1 practical ghost light; blue "leavy" drop (soft border)

Act One, Sc. 2:
(Corridor)

Ivanhoe score bound in red w/tie

Act One, Sc. 3:
(G&S Dressing Room)

Number one in brass; brown striped armchair (Gilbert); footstool to match chair; brown striped armchair (Sullivan); sideboard; stand w/umbrella & cane; music stand w/pencil; easel with wood framed picture; 2 round side tables; silver tea tray; silver tea pot; silver milk and sugar w/tongs; 2 china cups and saucers; 2 silver spoons; brass ashtray; small brass holder w/wooden matches; humidor w/cigars; glass water pitcher; 2 glass water tumblers; small fern in copper pot; 2 double wall sconces; 4 G&S framed show posters; wood plaque w/3 coat hooks; light switch; wood and gold framed picture (Ships); pirate flag on 6 ft. pole.

Act One. Sc. 4:
(Savoy Stage)

Iolanthe bench; Iolanthe arbour unit; 1 prop corset; 1 prop skirt (striped); 1 china tea cup w/water (no saucer)

Act One. Sc. 5:
(Green Room)

Ottoman w/2 pillows; brown straight back chair; white vanity w/padded corner & towel to mask; white straight back chair; 4 sets of 2-panel drapes; wooden framed picture of woman; brass coal box; silvery, blue vase w/pink flowers; silver mantel clock; 2 double wall sconces; 1 single wall sconce; make-up tray; 2 hair combs; several hair clips; corset/boot hook; 3 grease sticks; nail scissors; hand mirror; powder box; hair brush; number five in brass; light switch; 4 prop costumes on wood hangers; 1 empty wood hanger; 1 empty wood skirt hanger; 1 prop red kimono on wood hanger

Act One. Sc. 6:
(Savoy Stage)

Baton (Sullivan); tea cart; 2 china tea pots; 10 china cups and saucers; 10 silver spoons; silver sugar tongs; china milk and sugar; tea strainer; 1 china dessert plate; Mikado bridge; blue fabric "river"; (3) 14 in. fans (women); (3) 13 in. fans (men); (3) book piles w/cord hoops; sunshade - large tasseled (Alfred); prop "ugly wig" on block & stand.

Act One. Sc. 7:
(G&S Dressing Room)

Silver tray; 1 decanter w/brandy; 1 decanter w/port; 3
stemmed port glasses (crystal); 2 glass tumblers; 2
London newspapers (4 pgs ea.) (*The Times*)

Act Two. Sc. 1:
(Savoy Stage)

No new props.

Act Two. Sc. 2:
(G&S Dressing Room)

No new props.

Act Two. Sc. 3:
(Savoy Stage)

Tree stump w/flowers.

Act Two. Sc. 4:
(Savoy Stage)

No new props.

Act Two. Sc. 5:
(Corridor)

No new props.

Act Two. Sc. 6
(Corridor)

No new props.

Act Two. Sc. 7
(Savoy Stage)

Vinyl Mikado river (in 2 parts); (1) 8 in. wood carved fan
(Rosina); (3) 14 in. fans (women); (5) 15 in. red fans
(men); (2) 25 in. Mikado fans; (1) 9 in. umbrella
(Alfred)

PERSONAL PROPS

GILBERT:

Letter ("Dear Gilbert"); walking cane; small notebook
w/page torn out (names written on page: Maud Reilly,
Harriet Fleming, Emma Lane, Clarissa Carpenter)
(set in right vest pocket of street clothes); brown
leather wallet w/5 pound note (set in left breast inside
jacket pocket of street clothes); black leather wallet
w/notepad & pencil (set in left breast inside pocket of
tails jacket); 5 pound note in right pant's pocket of
street clothes.

SULLIVAN:

Letter ("Dear Sullivan"); monocle; *Ivanhoe* score (red
bound, tied in bow).

ALFRED:

Silver top cane.

KITTY:

Note (piece of paper).

CELLIER:

"Review Score"; 2 batons (1 preset in pit; 1 preset in
dressing room to carry on); rehearsal schedule (set in
pit).

RUTLAND:

Iolanthe coronet.

COURTICE:

Iolanthe coronet.

GEORGE:

Monocle in pocket of jacket; pince-nez attached to jacket lapel; wire rimmed glasses; Ko-ko glasses (black frames).

ROSINA:

Carpet bag; black covered parasol; *Iolanthe* crown (fx); *Iolanthe* wand w/battery pack.

SYBIL:

Iolanthe crown (fx); *Iolanthe* wand w/battery pack.

JESSIE:

Iolanthe crown (fx); *Iolanthe* wand w/battery pack.

PROPS PRESET LIST

PRESET TOP OF SHOW:

(On Stage)   Upright piano-USR on spikes - keys DS
                  1 Bentwood chair - DS of piano
                  Pirate set piece - USL - on stage
                     (Carpenters)
                  ghost light - USC - on stage (Electrics)
                  2 non-practical pinrails SR & SL - pins
                     US
                  1 Baton (Sullivan) on conductor's stand in
                     pit

                  1 Rehearsal schedule on conductor's stand
                     in pit

GILBERT'S PROLOGUE WAGON:

                  Preset position DSR (Carpenters)
                  Carpet on wagon
                  Brown upholstered armchair - on spike
                  Footstool to match chair - DSR of chair
                  Oval occasional table - CL of chair
                     w/small nail for cane rest on stage
                     w/black telephone, gold ornate clock
                     (attached), brass ash tray (attached)
                     cigar box (attached); ink well (attached)
                  Canterbury w/newspapers (dressing) - SR
                     of chair
                  Fern on gold stand

S.R. PROP TABLE:

(In wings)   Handled vase w/yellow flowers
                  Costume prop vest
                  Silver tray w/doily
                  2 glass decanters (1) with port; (1) with

whiskey
2 whiskey glasses (water tumblers)
3 stemmed port glasses
2 London newspapers (*The Times* w/4
    sections each)
2 spears
Mirror

SMALL PROP TABLE SR:

(On false deck)

(2) 14 in. fans (Sybil & Jessie)
(3) 13 in. fans (Rutland, Courtice,
    George)
(3) book piles w/belt loops
Deck of cards
Blindfold
Blue fabric *Mikado* "river"
(2) bolts for *Iolanthe* arbour
Sm. umbrella

SR OFF STAGE AREA:

(On false deck)

(2) costume rack w/:
    3 Bobby hats on top (att.)
    2 Beefeater hats on top (att.)
    2 Beefeater uniforms (on wooden
        hangers)
    Pirate costume bag w/5 big filler
        hangers
#2 Skip (single lock)
Sword in scabbard w/belt - in skip
Mikado bridge USR (2 pieces) w/2 drop
    bolts
Practical door slam unit (used in I,7)
Iolanthe arbour unit USR in store position

G&S DRESSING ROOM WAGON:

(In store position USR out of track)

> (1) brown striped armchair SR
> (1) brown striped armchair (SL w/ match
>   strike USR armchair
> (1) footstool (matching armchairs) at SL
>   chair
> Music stand - SU of SR chair
> Easel w/wood framed picture (UL of SR
>   chair
> Cane/umbrella stand w/ 1 of each - US of
>   SL chair
> (1) small side table - SR of SL chair
>   w/humidor:
> > brass ashtray w/water (attached)
> > small brass holder (attached)
> >   w/wooden matches
> > cigar clipper
>
> Sideboard against US wall w/glass pitcher
>   (w/water); 2 glass tumblers w/doily
>   under
> Small fern in copper pot - under easel
> 2 double wall sconces (each side of
>   sideboard)
> 4 G&S framed show posters:
> > *HMS Pinafore* SL wall
> > *Mikado* SL wall
> > *Patience* SLC wall
> > *Iolanthe* SRC wall
>
> Wood plaque w/3 coat hooks US door
>   onstage
> Light switch (in up position) DS door
>   onstage
> Wood and gold framed picture (ships)
>   above sideboard
> Number on in brass - on off stage side of

door
Pirate flag on 6 ft. - US preset position
Pirate sword belt
Pirate pistol
Dressing room pinned at door step
Check door knob

SULLIVAN'S PROLOGUE WAGON:

Preset position DSL (Carpenters)
Carpet on wagon
Green upholstered chair - on spike
Folding screen pinhinged to wagon - US of
    chair
Tall square occasional table - UR of chair
            w/ brass pot on legs (attached)
            oriental vase on stand w/white
                flowers (attached)
            oriental statue of man (lower
                shelf)
Small square table - DL of chair
            w/telephone   with   practical
clicking arm

SL PROP TABLE:

Silver tray service w/ silver tea pot
            w/ hot tea
            silver milk pitcher w/milk
            silver sugar bowl w/cubes & tongs
            (2) silver spoons
            (2) china cups w/saucers
Ornate cane (Rutland)
(3) envelopes w/letters inside (Rutland)
Section of red apple (Rutland)
Clipboard and papers (cast list &
    schedules) w/pencil
Clipboard and papers (cast list) w/pencil

(Gilbert)
Carpet bag w/wood handles (Sybil)
Cloth shopping bag (Jessie)
The Leader newspaper w/4 section (p.3 has
    picture of "Three Little Maids"
Make-up case (Violet)
Mikado fans:
>   (2) 25 in Mikado fans (Mikado)
>   (4) 15 in. Red fans (mens)
>   (3) 14 in. fans (women)
>   (1) 8 in. wooden carved fan
>   (Rosina)

Large umbrella (Alfred)

SMALL SL PROP TABLE:

(On false deck)
>   Throat sprayer
>   Blue leavy drop (soft border)
>   (2) Prop corsets
>   (1) Prop skirt (striped)
>   Prop "ugly wig" on block & stand
>   (Rosina)
>   (1) China tea cup (no saucer) w/water

SL OFF STAGE AREA:

(On false deck)
>   #1 Rack w/hooks on one end
>>   Pink academic robe (Durward)
>>   Pink academic robe (Courtice)
>>   (9) prop filler costumes
>>   Pink academic robe (Jessie)
>>   Pink academic robe (Sybil)
>>   Pink academic robe (Violet)
>>   Pink academic robe (Rutland)
>>   Mirror on other end
>>   (3) wig blocks on top (attached)

w/ 3 drag wigs w/hats attached
(blond - close to hook end of two
red - close to mirror end of two
brunette - center (single)
Lace hankie on top beside red wig

#1 Skip (double lock) w/
jester stick,
tamborine,
scroll (rolled from bottom)

(3) Bentwood chairs - preset position USL
on back of green room unit

Tea cart w/:
white cloth (on top)
(2) china tea pots w/hot tea
china milk & sugar w/tongs
10 china cups & saucers
10 silver tea spoons
Iolanthe bench - US of tea cart

Iolanthe bench - US of tea cart
(2) pieces vinyl "river" USR &
USL - US false deck, DS of US
ground row
(1) 14 in fan (womans) - preset
quick change booth

GREEN ROOM WAGON:

Preset position USL out of track (folded)
Carpet flap up - hooked (fireplace)
Ottoman w/2 pillows (in store position)
Vanity - hinged to wall SL leg only
w/make-up tray - nail buff
2 hair combs
several hair clips
corset/boot hook
3 grease sticks
Sm. nail scissors

Hand mirror
Hair brush
Powder box
Prop *Iolanthe* wig on block & stand
    (attached)
Padded DSL corner masked by sm. towel
    attached
White straight back chair at vanity
Drapes doorway C - preset open
Drapes doorway SR vanity - preset open
Drapes doorway SL vanity - preset closed
Brown straight back chair - hinged US to
    wall
4 prop costumes on wooden hangers
    (attached)
1 wooden shirt hanger
1 wooden hanger (set for Violet's coat
    during Act I)
1 red prop kimono - on wooden hanger
Number five in brass offstage side of door
Light switch - onstage side - SR of door
Wood frame picture of woman above
    fireplace
Brass coal box hinged to wall SR of
    fireplace
Silvery blue vase w/pink flower SL on
    mantle
Silvery clock - SR on mantle (attached)
(2) double wall sconces - each side of
    fireplace
(1) wall sconce - over vanity

About the Playwright

Ken Ludwig was born in 1950 in York, PA., and was educated at Haverford College, Harvard Law School, and Trinity College, Cambridge University. His plays include DIVINE FIRE; JOY IN MUDVILLE; POSTMORTEM; SULLIVAN & GILBERT (produced at the Kennedy Center & at the National Arts Center of Canada, where it was voted Best Play of the Year); and LEND ME A TENOR.

LEND ME A TENOR was produced in London by Andrew Lloyd Webber's Really Useful Co., and was nominated for the Olivier Award. It opened on Broadway in March 1989 and was nominated for seven Tony Awards, including Best Play. In addition to winning two Tonys, it won four Drama Desk Awards and three Outer Critics Circle Awards. It has been performed throughout the world in eight languages.

Mr. Ludwig is married and lives in Washington, D.C., where he divides his time between writing and practicing law with the firm of Steptoe & Johnson.

OTHER TITLES AVAILABLE FROM SAMUEL FRENCH

FALSETTOS
William Finn and James Lapine

Musical / 2m, 2f / Combined Interior

Music and Lyrics by William Finn. Book by William Finn and James Lapine. A seamless pairing of March of the Falsettos and Falsettoland, acclaimed off Broadway musicals written nearly a decade apart, Falsettos won 1992 Tony Awards for best book and musical score. It is the jaunty tale of Marvin who leaves his wife and young son to live with another man. His ex wife marries his psychiatrist, and Marvin ends up alone. Two years later, Marvin is reunited with his lover on the eve of his son's bar mitzvah, just as AIDS is beginning its insidious spread.

"Exhilarating and heartbreaking.... Falsettoland gains exponentially in power by being seen only 15 minutes, instead of 9 years, after the first installment."
– *The New York Times*

"A masterly feat of comic storytelling and ... visionary musical theater."
– *Variety*

OTHER TITLES AVAILABLE FROM SAMUEL FRENCH

ANGRY HOUSEWIVES
A.M. Collins and Chad Henry

Musical / 4m, 4f / Various sets
Bored with their everyday lives and kept in insignificance by their boyfriends/husbands, these are four angry women. They try a number of outlets, but nothing suits until one of them strikes a chord on her guitar and suggests that they form a punk rock group to enter the upcoming talent show at the neighborhood punk club. Their group "The Angry Housewives," enter and win. This genial satire of contemporary feminism ran for ages in Seattle and has had numerous successful productions across the country.

"The show is insistently outrageous, frequently funny, occasionally witty and altogether irresistible."
– *Seattle Times*

OTHER TITLES AVAILABLE FROM SAMUEL FRENCH

THE SPITFIRE GRILL
Music and Book by James Valcq
Lyrics and Book by Fred Alley
Based on the film by Lee David Zlotoff

Musical Drama / 3m, 4f / Unit Set

A feisty parolee follows her dreams, based on a page from an old travel book, to a small town in Wisconsin and finds a place for herself working at Hannah's Spitfire Grill. It is for sale but there are no takers for the only eatery in the depressed town, so newcomer Percy suggests to Hannah that she raffle it off. Entry fees are one hundred dollars and the best essay on why you want the grill wins. Soon, mail is arriving by the wheelbarrow full and things are definitely cookin' at the Spitfire Grill.

"An abundance of warmth, spirit and goodwill!...Some of the most engaging and instantly infectious melodies I've heard in an original musical in some time."
– *USA Today*

"A soul satisfying...work of theatrical resourcefulness. A compelling story that flows with grace and carries the rush of anticipation. The story moves, the characters have many dimensions and their transformations are plausible and moving. The musical is freeing. It is penetrated by honesty and it glows."
– *The New York Times*